GARBAGE BEAT

Twelve years of entertainment journalism, a lifetime as a manoranjan junkie. Richa Lakhera has worked for years as an entertainment journalist in prominent national news channels. She believes that you should accept your most demented thoughts, fears and fantasies. This is her first book.

GARBAGE BEAT

Richa Lakhera

HarperCollins *Publishers* India
a joint venture with

THE
INDIA
TODAY
GROUP

New Delhi

First published in India in 2012 by
HarperCollins *Publishers* India
a joint venture with
The India Today Group

ISBN: 978-93-5029-397-3

2 4 6 8 10 9 7 5 3 1

HarperCollins *Publishers*
A-53, Sector 57, Noida, Uttar Pradesh 201301, India
77–85 Fulham Palace Road, London W6 8JB, United Kingdom
Hazelton Lanes, 55 Avenue Road, Suite 2900, Toronto, Ontario M5R 3L2
and 1995 Markham Road, Scarborough, Ontario M1B 5M8, Canada
25 Ryde Road, Pymble, Sydney, NSW 2073, Australia
31 View Road, Glenfield, Auckland 10, New Zealand
10 East 53rd Street, New York NY 10022, USA

Typeset in 11.5/15 Adobe Jenson Pro
InoSoft Systems Noida

Printed and bound at
Thomson Press (India) Ltd.

*To the exceedingly exceptional and
brilliant television and print journalists
on the fiercely competitive entertainment beat.*

3...2...1... and Cue

This adrenalin rush is potent fuel for the heart pounding down panic street at 200 turbo knots. Hey bhagwan, hey Ganapati, bachao. Help me! They are watching... wishing for an on-air malfunction. My tongue is glued to the roof of my mouth, my teeth remain stubbornly stuck together and my guts are reduced to a mass of quivering jelly.

As I watched my TV life flash before me, I reminded myself that this was the moment I had been waiting for. My very own TV show. I told myself that it would make the double shifts, guilt trips and all the arse-licking worth it.

In a few minutes I was slotted to go live with a new entertainment show that had been hyped up with slick promos and cross-channel publicity donuts for weeks. The hitch being that my show was on the verge of becoming a still-born statistic. I was about to be publicly annihilated, consigned to TV-trash, a blooper, a cipher, a nullity, worse still, a non-entity.

There was no space in 'Unity', the virtual infinite universe that stores our TV footage. It had just tanked. A small technical problem had crashed the system and stalled smooth rendering of the story packages. Huge quantities of video content needed to be deleted from the server on an urgent basis, before anything could be published and aired.

'The engineers are at it,' an indifferent voice whispered into my earpiece, four words tailor-made to send my panic buttons on overdrive.

'Fuck. I am going to perish publicly.' My voice sounded hollow in static-sphere.

'Please don't overreact.' For the production control room (PCR) it was just another day of routine pandemonium. Chiki, my online editor, had stopped taking my calls, probably for the best. We would be on air in four minutes. I was living every producer's nightmare—seconds left to go, with no story to show.

I had to calm my frayed nerves.

'Laila, we don't have your first segment.'

'Shit.' All the glib talk, the gush and prattle of pre-show hoopla had been reduced to this, a last-minute sputter? I took a quick look at the reflection staring back at me from the studio mirror that the much-harried working-double-shift studio assistant was holding up. Then I put on my best on-air smile.

'Hey, what's the verdict on the 2G case? We will go to cover it if the lawyer holds a presser,' a news producer on standby in the PCR broke in.

'Okay, Laila, newsy day today, be ready in case we crash out from your show into news,' I was officially informed.

'Would Morani's lawyer do a symsat after the phono?'

A commanding voice from another planet boomed into the fly-like earpiece, a small metallic gadget comfortably lodged inside my right ear. 'Laila, move *right*.' It was the floor manager. 'Pan the camera a bit to the left... thoda right... yes, yes. Okay, hold!'

There I stood, perched on a small wooden riser, my petite four-feet-eleven-inch frame stretched to five feet one inch. Metal monsters shrieked.

Hey, thanks for blasting my cochlea to outer space. That bitch was gonna bust my eardrums! The scary thought popped into my head when a grating voice rasped into the earpiece, now gradually sinking deep into the folds of my right ear.

'Kautilya babe, ask her to say something for levels.'

'Laila, say something for levels,' Kautilya screeched.

'Can I get my output?' I asked.

'Give Laila her output on AUX 3. *Fix* Laila's shot. Zoom out. Laila, we will mix OTS *live*.'

The screen of the giant PGM-plasma flickered on and I found myself staring into my favourite gold-speckled designer fuschia bustier; the backless top in size two with a flattering silhouette had cost a bomb but had been made affordable by the sizeable anchor wardrobe reimbursement component allotted to me, now that I had my own show.

The show that I had landed only after seventeen auditions and ten mocks. Latika, the resident sex-bomb of my channel, and inarguably one of the most attractive journos in the television industry, had also tried for this spot. Over-enthu Indu, superhack and resident eager beaver, had also made a pitch. Not that I had anything against them, but what the heck, I wanted my own show so bad I could taste it. And I had slogged like a bitch for two shifts every day, stretching to three, to get the concept in place. Bunny, the entertainment editor and my supreme boss, enjoyed our little efforts at one-upmanship to impress her, and let us carry on for her amusement. Why she finally gave me the show remains a mystery, but I think in the end she just wanted to get me off her back.

'Give me graphics. Oye, Binny, couldn't you get me the latest grab of Shah Rukh Khan? This damn picture is so outdated! Shah Rukh lost these spring-chicken cheeks like a hundred years back, ya!'

Inside my right ear, a mumble followed by a shouting match broke out between graphics designer Binny and the studio director.

'What do you mean, the entertainment editor did *not* give you Shah Rukh's grab? Have you heard of Google, sweetie pie? Just Google and get Shah Rukh's latest picture, dude,' and in the same breath,

'Laila, say something for levels… give her the foldback,' the studio director said.

The OTS flickering on the screen caught my attention. It had a very cocky grab of Shah Rukh Khan in his long-haired post-*Don* avatar, split with a beaming and colourful Amitabh Bachchan from his *Budhha Hoga Tera Baap* days. A text screamed *King Kaun* in bold red even as a dramatic blue electric bolt tore across the faces of Shah Rukh and Bachchan.

'Do colour correction. Please fix Bachchan's shot. It's white beard and black hair, people,' she screamed.

As the PCR tried to fix the colour of Bachchan's beard, I took in the new show backdrop: A beautified set complete with kitschy cut-glass hangings on one side, and a huge plasma TV on the other. My show was titled *Filmy Masti*, which sounded quite corny but it was given by the editor, and I was just the reporter, anchor, producer, script writer, what did I know?

'Shove Shah Rukh up, move Bachchan a bit down!' boomed the studio director, queen of her console, in the dimly lit PCR.

'Put another RF mike on the anchor for backup. I do *not* want that Rene-wala scene again just in case this one hangs. Gosh, can someone patch the frigging radio frequency mike on her, guys?'

'Badee director banee firtee hai—such crappy attitude these women from swanky-phanky journo schools have. Bhaiyya, I have learnt on the job.' Pandeyji, the chief studio assistant, shrugged his chubby frame and grumpily directed his second-in-line assistant, a new trainee, one who was very much in awe of the mysterious-looking stainless-steel equipment in the studio. The gigantic army of cameras, the massive portable camera crane or JIB swaying from side to side, straight out of a *Transformers* set, deep black holes when switched off and throbbing with psychedelic life when switched on, *that* was the forbidding technical setup. A JIB basically looks like a camera fucking a fifty-foot construction crane.

'Laila, your first VT package is *still* not here. Should we take Vivek before Salman?' the director blasphemed, even as Ma Simmy Chabbra, the resident chakra healer, walked in to bless the studio.

'I cannot start my first show with Vivek Oberoi.' I was close to tears. I could already see Lattoo and Indu smirking, 'We told you so.' And Bunny hollering, 'Kiss your show goodbye, dumbass.'

'Babe, nothing is in… you just have three minutes… we take the second segment first or there is *no* show!'

Chiki, Chiki, are you fucking sleeping or drunk?

'Shit. Okay. Then start with Vivek Oberoi instead of Shah Rukh Khan,' I choked.

'*Whose mobile is on in the studio?* Where do these kids come from? *No* studio etiquette.' The intern jumped guiltily, grabbed her mobile and killed it.

'The plasma is not working. Is the plasma *not* working? *Fix it, fix it!* Why is the bubble skewed? Pandeyji, please adjust the chroma. *Why* is there a reflection? *Who* is moving in the studio in front of the plasma? *Check,* are the babys off? Go light on the blue dimmer—only cold lights, we can try variations on JIB, MCU and OTS.' The director belted out last-second instructions. .

'Okay, Laila! Your Shah Rukh-vs-Amitabh package is here—ready to go.'

Obviously Chiki had just managed a miracle and published the first story.

A couple of hundred light years later…

'Shah Rukh is *married*! Second is on its way… Okay, Laila! Salman is *married*. We have both Shah Rukh and Salman packages. Both VTs married. Guys, change in run order again. *Shove Vivek down,* get Shah Rukh and Salman VTs right on top.'

The relief I felt was orgasmic. I wanted to hug Chiki frigging Bose.

Beam me up, Scotty! I was sure Rehan would be watching my first live show. Wherever he was, I hoped he had managed to get to a TV in time. He had promised to text me his first reaction.

'Laila, coming to you on the JIB in five.'

'Laila, we may crash out in case we get the verdict in Mumbai.'

'Laila, there is a cabinet meeting on petrol price roll back, we may go to it if there is breaking news.'

'*Standby*.'

'Laila, are we ready to roll?'

'Yes!' I said, even as my mobile vibrated with Rehan's *best of luck*.

'Roll bumper, roll bumper… *Why* don't you send it asap?'

'Bumper fade… audio up… music up.'

'Go viz.'

'Graphics roll.'

'Standby.'

'3—2—1.'

'And cue.'

TV journalism is a bit like magic. Anyone who has gone through this particular trauma of 'collapsing Columbus', 'server hanging up', 'ISIS shutdowns', 'tapes totally shot', 'non-aligning tracks', 'crashing systems', 'Unity tanking up', 'rendering errors', 'corrupting files', 'zero-speed FTP trauma', 'glitched tapes' or 'rustling mikes' knows the futility of trying to hold together a pack of falling cards.

The dependence of TV on the scientific is absolute. And since human factors cannot be neglected in planning machinery or safeguarding oneself against technical errors, TV journalism, from conception to delivery, is entirely an affair of faith.

It was a tightly concealed box that opened to a tiny cylindrical sky. That's the best way to describe where Chiki and I stood. We had reason to. Chiki had stumbled onto the only place in EMTV where she could smoke in peace, and I could de-static-fy—our top-secret, smoke-filled, static-free hideout, which Chiki had managed to find behind the fifth-floor toilet. And we would do whatever it took to keep it that way. Chiki was violating EMTV's strict commandment: 'Thou shalt not smoke in peace in here'. But I did not hold it against her if that was what it took for her to send a reasonably coherent show on air. Lately I had taken to squeezing into the cramped space with her, inhaling second-hand smoke, finding strange peace in getting choked and gassed.

'Laila, I have finished my stock of ciggies. You got my Dunhill from Rehan?' she asked.

'You know he has stopped, babe,' I said, furiously exchanging SMSes with Rehan.

o gawd. I m scrwd, I sent.

you rocked, he sent.

i wil b floggd, I sent.

they loved you, he sent.

k ciao gt black swan tickts xxtra chilly mmos, I sent.

'Even Red and White would do… I am suffering here, lady,' Chiki persisted. I ignored her. I was suffering too. My legs were killing me from standing on the wooden studio riser for over an hour, my throat was sore, my ears bruised by the talkback, my head numb, but all she wanted was her ciggies.

'You had also promised to get me the Camel menthols,' she hissed petulantly, crowding me into a corner with a nasty look.

No one else came to the hideout. I was allowed on occasion, but truly welcomed only if I came armed with Dunhills and Marlboros. The floor was littered with what Chiki had smoked over the months mixed with pigeon shit, and a poster of her favourite Bollywood actor Amar Kapoor. We had pigeons for company who hated us to begin with but eventually accepted us in the face of our dogged persistence. They even stopped shitting on the Amar Kapoor poster after a while.

Chiki was desperately craving her nicotine fix after the nightmare the avid newscutter machines had put her through. Bunny would have scalped her hide if the stories had not come on time. Chiki was sure it was the squeaky-clean journo school kids who made her look so bad in front of Bunny.

'Chiki, are you also trying to get us a notice from the broadcasting fucking ministry? Were you fucking drunk when you were editing? How could you let the damn cuss words of that arsehole star go on air?' Bunny had yelled.

'Remove the three son-of-a-bitches, one breast, two bums, a sixty-nine, two dogs, three maadarchods, two saalas and two chutiyas. Fucking remove them from the chunk. Before H. Raami loses it. And thank these new kids, or you would have been kissing your lousy journo life's arse goodbye. This is EMTV News, not MTV Roadies, you idiot. We are a family channel. We don't cuss on air.'

Bunny had not even spotted the cuss words in the actor's interview. It was one of the health- and morally-conscious, just-out-of-journo-school brigade who seemed to infest EMTV nowadays.

'What are they teaching these pretentious kids nowadays? Don't abuse. Say fish for fuck. Say no to red meat. Go vegan. Don't use polybags. Save the butterflies,' Chiki hammered melodramatically. 'Oh fish, Chiki, you don't wanna come for the "City for Citizen" campaign? Why don't you pitch in? Shoot me while going to the frigging plug-the-ozone-hole event in my AC SUV. Oh fish, let me check my brand-new visiting card made from scented paprika roots, it is somewhere in my genuine leather pouch. No, I can't come to your pad today, ya. I am too busy making the world go healthy!'

'"City for Citizen" is big, dude,' I ventured listlessly.

'Are you serious? Don't they have a life? Probably the only ungodly thing that goes into their mouths ever is, what, bubble gum or something! Now what would they think if they got to know of the number of ungodly things that have gone into my mouth?' Chiki smiled wickedly. I refrained from commenting.

'Well, fuck them. Fuck their tofu and dexedrine-soaked celery sticks. Spirulina and tuna and beans and seeds. Fuck their ginseng-stuffed health food. Fuck their organic hot chocolate. And double fuck their grass-fed beef, what the fuck is that?' Truth was I couldn't care less but Chiki was pissed that the chits hissed at her for her inorganic habits.

'A juicy buttery steak with lots of extra garlic, butter and French fries and make it a large Coke, please!' Chiki would shout in the café to piss them off. She felt some violent emotion towards the tchhhtchhhing army who looked down on her smoking and singing. Just like her mother. Chiki thought of her mother and took a long, tortured drag. Her mother Mrs Chitra Bose, divorcee and ex-beauty queen who lived with her son in Bangalore's MG Road, was threatening to come to Delhi ever since she had found the cigarette stubs in the commode from her last stopover. That would never do.

Chiki Bose had fucked up again and was pissed at Bunny for taking her case in front of the interns.

'Man, I have to get out of this psycho place. I will frigging do whatever it takes, dude,' she raged before heading back to the edit bay to chunk my *Filmy Masti* show.

Garbage Beat

So here I was, doing what was supposed to be my dream job with my dream channel, EMTV. It is the one place where entertainment journos have always wanted to be since the day they wanted to be journos. The colossal thirty-two-storey yellow and green glass building that blocked out most of the sun for the major part of the day in Delhi's Jhandewalan Marg is the stuff I dreamt of for the longest time. I used to beg Rehan to slow down the car whenever we crossed the EMTV building so that I could stare at the glittering glass façade. Rehan would get pissed at the number of times I made him stop the car at the intersection opposite the EMTV building to grab a Coke from the roadside paan stall. It was an excuse to stop and ogle at the building, and also at the smart-looking boys and girls who came out for some friendly banter, screaming 'Munna, ek dena' at the stall guy.

I desp...
partially...
carelessly...
on their p...
was it easy...
fact that h...
colleagues l...
and engine...
on doing so...
Papa was sh...
was earning...
a local TV c...
Ma too was ... and embarrassed.

Since the job with the television...
about, and quickly proved dan...
on, I took up a job from 7 a...
and then returned to th...
shift. I actually sur...
my teaching job...
papa convi...

As I...
edu...

But whether papa and ma liked it or not, the world had started changing at a very fast pace in 2003. And with it, my life. Indian television had begun mutating into the huge monster it is today. Of course, I had no way of knowing then that TV would start spawning a whole new breed of demi-gods with legions of worshippers. All that mattered to me was that television seemed to be the only place where anything remotely exciting was happening. For those on the outside, it was not that big a deal when I joined the relatively unknown TV channel as an underpaid, overworked, over-enthusiastic, over-ambitious, hyperactive, wide-eyed intern in its Delhi bureau. I was just one of the twenty-five trainees TV India had hired for the daily news and features channel, to cut costs and get the next bulletin on air. Basically, we were the labour force, but it was big stuff for me, a twenty-two-year-old with stars in my eyes.

was nothing to write home
gerously inadequate to survive
.m. to 2 p.m. as a teacher in a school
e TV station to work a 2 p.m. to 11 p.m.
ived my early years in television because of
. My family was horrified. For the longest time
nced himself that it was a passing fad.

was saying, journalism was taboo for the respectably
cated middle-class family. Looking at my determination,
my father lamented, 'Of what use is your first class in MSc
physics from Delhi University's Hindu College?'

'Par papa...'

'Of what use are your outstanding grades and scholarship
in BEd?'

'But papa...'

To give the devil his due, it's not as if I did not try. I taught
10+2 physics. I gave pre-medical tuitions (700 bucks an hour).
But it made me gag. I did not want to spend my productive days
lost in the wilderness of the Indian education system. I toyed
with the idea of being in the IFS, as it seemed pretty glamorous.
I started studying for the civils, but it hit me soon enough that I
was transforming into the most miserable person in the world.
My disdain for all things respectable and safe was disconcerting
for an ambitious father who, being in the civil services himself,
had planned a picture-perfect civil services life for his daughter,
preferably with a perfect civil services husband.

But I did not want to spend my life going through files to
install a nullah in a village, or cover a manhole in a city, or worse,
be a babu's wife. It was just not glamorous.

Nor did the thought of peering into other people's diseases give me a high, so an MBBS was definitely out. I could hear the grumbling from my relatives—near as well as distant.

'Gaddhey mein jaaogee—you will end up in a ditch,' they always said.

'Think of your father. He had such dreams for you.'

My mother blamed my father for spoiling me. 'You never even let her inside the kitchen,' she wailed. Papa in turn accused poor ma of turning a blind eye to my school teachers' constant complaints that I was too nosy for my own good. He even fished out an old report card in which my least favourite teacher, Mrs Burns, had called me an incorrigible liar prone to spilling secrets, especially the most sacred ones.

Papa, himself a PhD from London School of Economics and an economic advisor in the Indian ministry, did not hold journalists in high regard. He called journalism the first option of the idiot, the last option of the greedy and the only option of the rascal. But such glowing testimonials only served to increase the charm of the forbidden domain.

I was ecstatic when I got my first job as trainee reporter at a newly launched national TV network, which had just been set up by a business group. The group's main business remained a mystery to me but Rehan was a dear and Googled everything about the company to help me get through the interview. I had already started imagining the rush of my first byline, my first piece-to-camera, my first live on-air broadcast, my first interview.

But my first memorable TV moment included none of this; it had nothing to do with television. It was an almost other-worldly encounter with Amitabh Bachchan. I saw Amitabh

Bachchan up close for the first time on my first day at the job—tall and lanky, in white kurta pyjama and his trademark white beard—and I was ecstatic. I actually mistook him for a life-size cutout for a moment. But then the cutout smiled and my head reeled.

'Amit sir yahaan bahut aatey hai. He is like family. Very close to the boss!' hissed a gentleman standing next to me. He was waiting for his turn to do a sashtaang dandvat pranaam in front of the tall superstar. As Amitabh sir accepted his pranaam, devoted fans and employees started queuing up for their turn. I felt someone prod me from behind to be ready to go next. I held out my hand, hoping a handshake would be an acceptable alternative to a dandvat pranaam. Mercifully, a huge entourage swept Bachchan away, and I did not have to go through the acid test. I don't think Amitabh Bachchan even saw my outstretched hand.

'Madam, you are part of family. You and Amitabh Bachchan now belong to the same parivaar,' he informed me magnanimously.

Amitabh Bachchan and I belonged to the same family! Had a nice ring to it.

Mr Prabu, my very first editor, was a sharp man with an intimidating demeanour. He left no stone unturned in grilling me during the interview.

'So you have *zero* TV experience?' He stressed on zero.

'I have done a news internship in TV India.'

'But no practical knowledge of live news?' he asked.

'I have done feature reports. I have worked as assistant copy editor.'

'Have you anchored? Will you anchor weather?'

'What? No! I want to do entertainment.'

'Who the hell wants to be a tabloid hack? Entertainment is not journalism. It's just peep show! You can join news as an intern?'

'But sir, I will not join at less than assistant producer, entertainment,' I said desperately, hoping that there were marks for peskiness.

'Okay, it's all yours. It's still the garbage beat, that's not going to change.' He gave up too soon, or perhaps it was my lucky day.

I found myself in an office resembling a community hall. It looked as if some government babus had deserted the space in a hurry and a TV station had sprung up overnight. Lots of computers arranged in neat rows in a gigantic dorm-like hall, cold editors, tired sub-editors, intimidating special correspondents, male anchors for serious news looking as if they had been airbrushed, and female anchors for entertainment, sports and weather, sizing me up from head to toe. Unfriendly reporters pounded away furiously at their battered computer keyboards, their killer stories hoping to make their bylines bigger, and get more recognition than the brand itself. Then there were the over-friendly junior hacks with a desperate air, trying to look more important than they actually were in the newsroom. There were no pretentious swanky setups or technical gizmos. Just a huge hall punctured at regular intervals by mini-sized cubes called edit bays, which were inhabited by uniformly obese (from sitting too much, I guess!) video editors and their huge old-fashioned cut-to-cut edit machines.

Every organization has its own rules. The ones that can't be broken and the ones that *shan't* be broken. The most important rule in this channel was to wish every colleague with the following gesture—right hand touching the left side of the chest with a little curtsy. This performance was expected every time someone sufficiently important in the parivaar arrived. You could spot the big bosses long before their mortal presence, from the way some hacks fell to the ground performing the dandvat pranaam.

But the real problem was that the place was not even close to a real newsroom—or what I had imagined a real newsroom would be like!

No reassuring sight of choleric and foul-mouthed editors.

No neurotic chain-smoking women hacks pushing their stories.

No one collapsing in a flood of tears.

No seriously snarling, barking and bullying producers giving reporters a dressing down. There was actually a news person whose only claim to reportage fame was that he had killed a tiger with his bare hands. The family had its priorities in place.

The proverbial final straw that led to a mass exodus of journalists was the atmosphere, which did not really condone sexual equality and frowned on aggressive women hacks. So the men sat in little men-groups, and the women sat in little women-groups. Within months, most of the journalists, including me, contemplated moving to greener pastures. In any case, I was in a hurry to get on with the real job of reporting in a real channel. It no longer mattered that Amitabh Bachchan and I were in the same parivaar.

What mattered was that my journey into journalism had begun. I learnt why a reporter was only a small cog in the giant news-wheel, along with an army of camerapersons, video editors, engineers, editorial, graphics, producers, make-up artists and technicians. I learnt about continuity and ad libbing and a type of camera shot known as noddies, piece-to-cameras or p-to-cs, two-way satellite data transceivers or symsats, archiving, deadlines and chromas.

The toil and trudge and plod of the early years soon gave way to push and hustle and dash after the stars. I learnt to have no qualms about flashing my press card to gain privileged access into the expensive lives of the superstars, feed on their vanity, puff up their quirks, play with their prejudices, fleece, plead, lie, pretend. Suck them dry of every nugget of interesting information, and then leave. I had started mutating into an incorrigible hack who would do whatever it took to get that story. After all, I had a greater responsibility in the newsy scheme of things.

I had still to learn that it was a 'privileged' hack who was actually *allowed* to practise the trade—the rest had the retainers' and management's eyes firmly fixed on their arses. I was ignorant of the infinite hours I would have to spend pursuing El Dorado leads, the colossal number of wasted hours waiting for daft celebrity-related stories. I was still to learn about the frustration of having your story dropped. The unending agonizing over the technicalities of broadcasting non-stop news, equipment going for a toss right before deadline, slow editors and uncooperative camerapersons, the wait in the sun and rain and cold weather for the one byte that would make a whale of a story. Of course, it would eventually be chopped to a one-minuter, or worse, dropped altogether.

I was still to learn just how unimportant the entertainment beat was in the scheme of things for a news channel. The bimbette babble between seriously important news makers such as Kalmadi, Modi, Pawar, Kani, Niira, Kasab and Gaddafi, Gadkari and Ramdev and, of course, Anna Hazare and Kejriwal.

All that I learnt in EMTV. Eyes wide open, I crashlanded into the war zone of daily news as an entertainment hack. The channel was housed on twenty-three floors in the tallest, fancy building in Delhi's Jhandewalan Marg. It was owned by a Mumbai-based gutkha king who gave up his plan of diversifying into kitchen masalas, and opened a national news channel on a whim. There are people like that, you know. Unless they do it to save taxes.

Anyway, once I was in, there was no turning back for me. Also, by that time, I had been assured that I had that particular *something* because of which I would not have to undergo any training, burn the midnight oil or network like a troll.

'You are photogenic!' And *that* was supposed to help me in TV town in some mysterious way.

Photogenic

Mirror mirror on the wall... who is the most photogenic of us all?

Being a TV journalist is not that big a deal. The romanticism goes out with the labour of ball-crushing daily reportage. TV journalism is not for the ra-ra girls—too haughty to be hungry, too vain to be ambitious, too hoity toity to dirty their hands. The vain, the boorish and the incompetent might stand a fighting chance but the faint-hearted should bail out now. Unless they are photogenic.

It should have helped people like Latika big time—being photogenic, that is.

When she sashayed into the café, usually at lunch time, conversation stopped midway, people gawked and men whistled. That day, Latika walked in to admiring glances from all the men and blatant stares from the two interns, and made a beeline for her favourite seat, one with the large French windows. Chiki and I were wolfing down mutton patties before roll time but Latika ignored us completely. She stood still; her favourite seat had been taken. Pouting, Latika looked around, batting her eyelashes, sending the men into collective spasms of idiocy. The seats were vacated in a jiffy. Basically, Lattoo had it in her to make the opposite sex act like morons. She had been told innumerable times that she had *it*. What she perhaps didn't get was why I got to anchor *Filmy Masti* instead of her.

'Yello, Laila! Nice going, ya, so pretty you were looking on air. All dolled up again?' Lattoo waved at me.

'Thnsk… I grjhmckd… thank Chiki and the editor, both were so good—' I said, gulping down my lunch.

'Stop your thank you speech, idiot. It's embarassing,' Chiki hissed at me, and left the café with a 'Ciaaaaaaao, beautiful' directed at Lattoo.

I knew Latika was perplexed by Bunny's decision to hand me the show, a show that was supposed to target a twenty-five-plus audience, mostly working males.

'What was the response like?' Lattoo asked.

'Too early for the numbers, na!' I tried to sound like a pro.

I am sure Lattoo did not like the feeling of having been superannuated by me, but she did not look particularly worried. Perhaps she had started accepting that she was out of favour with Bunny.

'Your scripts suck. Your style is flat, it's an obvious attempt at being smart, too formulaic,' Bunny had told her coldly in front of the whole desk.

'I cannot send you to interview the actors. You just do not know anything about Bollywood, do you? Have you any idea who Bimal Roy was? No, not the business guy. Do you even know who Guru Dutt was? He was no relation to Sanjay Dutt, you know.' There was no stopping Bunny…

'Tum shaadi kar lo. Don't let go of your British boyfriend. Marry him. Have nice little English kids. This teevee-sheevee is not for you, madam.' Bunny had started sending her to the boring director-producer shoots that no one really wanted to do. But Lattoo never complained. She was to interview Shyamu Sharma again. This was her fifth interview of the filmmaker and she had boasted that they were already on first-name basis. The thing was, Latika knew she had become the fallen star of the desk, when she failed to live up to Bunny's expectations. Or rather, when she decided to stop living up to her expectations and start doing something on her own. For, Lattoo had very different dreams for herself.

The Bolly Types

Every journalist preys on people's vanity... ignorance... loneliness... gaining their trust... betraying them without remorse...

— JANET MALCOLM

My desk was on the tenth floor of the EMTV building. Technically, EMTV starts from the tenth floor going right up to the thirty-second. The floors below us belong to assorted banks, travel agencies, notaries and a play school. Every morning, before my shift started at 4 a.m., I looked out of my green and yellow glassy enclosure and reminded myself that this was my dream job.

Of course, like every Bollywood reporter, I had a lot of other dreams. I dreamt of running after Salman, wooing Shah Rukh, understanding Aamir. I dreamt of following the love life of India's sweethearts Katrina, Ranbir, Dipika, Priyanka... and perhaps even dating some Bollywood baddies.

So, was it my love of Shah Rukh Khan that kept me going? Or did I fancy myself as one of the truth seekers, asking questions that should not have been asked? Or did I do it for that sexy story that would make the viewer stop and watch... when the music, the script, the graphics, the text, the voice-over, and the big story of the day came together in one giant orgasmic rush?

Or so I thought.

'What's the tearing hurry? You are doing entertainment only, yaar. Sorry, but I cannot spare an editor for you entertainment guys till 10 p.m.!' the Hindi output producer, sitting on her throne on the twenty-first floor, informed me when, after finishing my show, I happened to inquire about the entertainment edit schedule.

I was confronted by these newsy types every day. They populated three important floors from the nineteenth to the twenty-first. The Bolly types, or the Bollies—that was my desk—sat on the tenth floor, spliced between two toilets and the kitchen, the accounts, the travel and the guest desks. Also at a stone's throw from the EMTV main kitchen for staff and guests, in case I didn't mention. At least we got our coffee hot, we Bolly types consoled ourselves.

That's the way it was in EMTV. You could guess the importance of a particular denizen from the floor they inhabited.

So, gutkha king occupied the stratospheric five floors of the building, from the twenty-eighth to the thirty-second. We didn't know what these floors contained as we had never visited the ones above the twenty-seventh. The CEO, the VP, the associate VP and other management members inhabited the three floors between twenty-five and twenty-seven, and one of them also housed the conference rooms. The twenty-second floor through the twenty-fourth had a gym, a splash pool, a billiards room and a lounge, and also Ma Simmy Chabbra's reiki room. The news desks, news producers and city news reporters populated three floors, from the nineteenth to twenty-first. The nineteenth also had the special edit suites reserved exclusively for all-important foreign correspondents and super-pampered political reporters. Business, occupying the sixteenth, seventeenth and eighteenth floors, and sports, on the thirteenth, fourteenth and fifteenth, had their own make-up rooms. Floors eleven and twelve were inhabited by the features, documentaries, books and arts desks, which were also entertainment, but not really Bollywood. They got more respect than the Bolly types so they got two floors to themselves.

'File it if you must, Laila! Arrey, just give me a sexy "and finally" and don't bother to exceed one minute,' smirked a serious desk producer.

'Arrey, madam Lailaji, how is Mallika? Rakhi Sawant par no story today? Bipasha ke kya haal hai?' the Hindi news producer nudged me.

'Star News is running a Katrina lip-job VT. Can't we get something on actors' plastic surgeries for our show? Huh? Just a small two-minute VT? Huh, huh?' said the virago with a vertigo, sipping her twentieth cup of coffee.

'Parrrrrty in the day. Parrrrrty at night! Mazaaaa hai. Who did you meet last night?' This was the slimy lech from the eighteenth floor.

'Hi, sundari, let's run and do something dirrrty!' the stud-anchor from the twentieth floor drooled.

'Hey, I have heard that after John Abraham, Minissha Lamba is also insuring her butt?' one of the news anchors said suggestively.

'Ek chulbul kayee bulbul!' someone else retorted.

Lewd remarks, endless sarcasm and cynicism. Every Tom and Dick felt, no, totally believed, that entertainment reporters were there for their personal manoranjan too. A clichéd mindset had set the entertainment reporters apart from the rest of the news reporters, even in a serious channel like EMTV. Entertainment was like fast food—nice and easy—but providing no real nourishment. Lumped together as the Garbage Beat.

I must introduce you to the entertainment desk on EMTV now, the scumbags pounding the garbage beat.

Chiki: Fat then thin then fat. Chiki Bose seemed to swell or shrink two sizes every month. The neurotic out-of-control chain-smoking crazy Bollywood fan. Chiki had a very pretty face. She also had an attitude problem. There was a time long ago when she was Bunny's smoking buddy and the apple of her eye. That was before she arrived at the important Oscar ceremony edit shift totally stoned. That was before she slapped the guard of a hotel who wanted to carry out a routine security check on her bags. That was before she insisted on sleeping on a sofa in a five-star hotel lobby and had a fit when she did not get her one-on-one celebrity interview at a star-studded event. That was before she arbitrarily started dropping stories and changing run orders without informing anyone. Last time she had put in her resignation, the editor had refused to accept it. That was then.

Latika or Lattoo, as we loved to call her: Easily the most beautiful girl in the channel. One look at her stunning olive complexion and gorgeous brandy eyes and you knew why she got the job. She had actors making passes at her routinely. But the bitch thing was—she was as dumb as they got. There was a time when the editor almost declared her the new superstar.

Indu or Indumati: A hyperactive over-achieving aloe vera addict. She had devoted the best eighteen years of her life aggressively reporting different beats from sports, politics, business and health for different channels. How she finally ended up in entertainment remains a mystery. She lived in a three-bedroom flat in Noida, which she had purchased with her own money, as she liked to remind us. Older photographs of Indu, which I retrieved from the channel annals, revealed a happy-looking plump and pretty girl—a far cry from the unsmiling, ginseng-crunching woman, who at this moment was pounding a script into her computer opposite me, her biological clock going tick tock, tick tock. Her chief gripe was that even after nine years in the channel she had not been given her own show. Of late, Indu had refused to do page three type entertainment—she thought it beneath her. So the editor sent her for art exhibitions, music and dance shows and book launches whenever she could.

Arindam Gopalakrishnan, better known as Nandu: The thing about Nandu was that he stood up for himself and answered only to himself. Touching forty, he had managed to alienate many people with his sharp tongue. But of course, he was careful never to antagonize the biggies. He had the best of contacts, which he kept greedily to himself. Every night while we slogged at shoots and in the studio or edit rooms, Nandu would be at parties guzzling wine, downing meat kebabs or air-kissing till dawn. He never came to office before 3 p.m. and left by 7 p.m. He had a hit show and he was close to the bosses… the editor's bosses. He was also writing a bestseller and was in talks with a hot-shot publisher. I don't think the editor could do much about Nandu. Many felt that he was a phoney, but I had a strange admiration for him, which he took full advantage of by dumping his boring shoots on me.

Bunny: Bunny Chopra. Let's just say that before I met her I did not know one person could invoke such intense fear and raw hatred in so many people at the same time. I had to continually remind myself that she was just thirty-one years old.

As for me, it would take an entire book to get to know me.

I guess that's why I'm writing it.

Live Feed

> *Journalism requires a man or woman to be sound physically and alert mentally. It's not a profession for the weak. It will stand you in good stead if you can take verbal abuses of all sorts, without getting into a tizzy about it.*
>
> — ANONYMOUS

I parked my car in the rapidly filling parking lot of the city high court. There was an air of anticipation. Bollywood star Upendra, of debatable sexual orientation, was in the net for rape. He had allegedly raped his nineteen-year-old manservant in a drunken state. His wife had been visiting her parents during this misdeed.

It was early hours yet but the word had spread fast. The court premises had started packing up. Cars were trickling in one after the other—the mammoth media vans were the first to arrive. TV trucks and news crew jostled with crowds milling outside the court premises. Television channels' OB vans were struggling for prime spots. The place was teeming with camerapersons and OB assistants and engineers and reporters from national channels and local news cables, all bickering for the *best* spot. Production assistants had started laying down thick, mile-long cables that would send live feeds. It was going to be anything but a dull day.

'I am in a screw-the-world mood!' muttered Gaurav from X Channel, trying to locate his spot and unpacking his cables. 'Man, our life is so overrated.'

'That Ambika—you know, from Moon News, the one who does lifestyle—is getting married. I asked her what her guy does and she answered, "He lives in Golf Links." How uncomplicated! I want to be Ambika.' This came from Gogol. No one could ever make out whether he was serious or not, but I found his sense of the absurd endearing.

'Good for her. She has seen the light,' I said.

'I have a better idea—you know, north and south Korea are fighting,' Gaurav said. 'Let's chuck all this and just go, kuch to karengey, yaar, it's so exciting.'

'Yeh dekhiye. Yeh ek grenade fataa, yeh bomb fataa. Seriously, every agency will be after us. I will definitely volunteer *reporting live from GBD!*' said Gogol.

'It's GMZ,' I said.

'GMZ, GBD, whatever! Bhonsdi ke, it's so hot, ya, I am frying.'

It was the new circus in town. There were reporters in crisp cottons, all wired up and armed with their cameras, mikes, tape recorders, writing their piece-to-cameras, or speaking on their dictaphones. Not to mention a swelling crowd of onlookers loitering and gawking at the media walas. Just ordinary people revelling in all the action, as if waiting for the nautanki to begin. I had taken care to dress very news-reporter-like—a short red kurta and blue jeans, a liberal dose of black kohl and lip gloss—sober enough for news reporting, sexy enough for entertainment. 'Laila, are you going to cover IIFA in Amsterdam? What a super-sexy lineup—Shah Rukh, Salman, Katrina—I toh am going,' Gaurav beamed.

'Hey, I am also going!' slimy Saryu from T Channel announced grandly. 'But you guys always send that Nandu. He went for Cannes also. How come *you* never go?' she smirked.

Saali bitch.

'As it happens, I am going this time! Maybe we can shop for some nice clothes for you there!' I shot back cattily and moved in the direction of my spot, towards entry gate number one, followed by my six-feet-one-inch tall cameraman Vibheeshan. He was no ordinary cameraman. Vibheeshan's impressive biceps could support the monstrously heavy Ikegami camera in one hand without the help of a supporting stand—and that's quite a feat—yet he managed to give me the most steady shots. I hurried over to the nearest policeman and flashed my press card importantly.

'Excuse me, sir…'

'Madam, udhar hi rukiye.'

'Arrey, bhaisaab, yehi poochna hai… kab tak aayengey?'

'Please wait there only, madam… don't *interrupt* us. Wait there, wait, *waiyyt*! Don't disrupt us.'

Ya bugger. I can see you have a lot to do.

The phone beeped. It was Partho from the coordination desk. 'What have you got? Is he there?'

'No one has come yet, Partho,' I said.

'Surely you can give a pre-rec? Give us some meat masala, na.'

Bunny was hyperventilating. A bitchy piece-to-camera would keep Bunny sated for some time, I thought. That is, unless she saw another channel running something juicier and meatier.

I zeroed in on a quiet corner to establish my location, a generous visual of the court's distinctive red brick structure in the background. And lovely light, which you get only at a particular hour of the day in Delhi—perfect for the p-to-c, except for a baby-faced gent who stood between me and my spot.

'Sir, excuse me.'

Without moving an inch, the man turned to look at me blankly.

'Sir, can I shoot here?' I asked. 'I mean, the light is good here so…'

'Sir, the light is good here,' the man repeated after me.

'Excuse me, sir?' The chap was definitely mimicking me! Had I offended him?

'*Excuse me, sir,*' he repeated in a high-pitched voice and moved towards me. I was alarmed. Shit, where was the cameraman when I needed him?

Out of the blue, three men swooped down on the baby-faced gent.

'Sirji, there you are.'

'Sirji, let's go, the hearing has been postponed.'

'Sorry, madam, don't be afraid! Yeh aise hi hai,' they said, seeing my terrified expression.

'He has not been in a good frame of mind since his daughter committed suicide after she was raped, madam,' one of the men informed me.

'Oh, I am so sorry,' I said, stunned.

'She was raped by his driver, madam.' I listened, horrified, watching the blank eyes fixed on me.

'Madam, you from media? Which channel?' The baby-faced man's keeper stared goggle-eyed at the media card hanging from my neck. 'EMTV! Arrey, mera favourite channel! You are madam Lailaji. Aapko dekha hai. Your Bollywood show—*Raat Mein Masti!*'

'No, my show is *Filmy Masti*…'

The men exchanged notes on my show and seemed to have forgotten about the man in their care.

I tried to stir up an appropriate response, but Bunny was going ballistic SMSing about the footage, and my cameraman Vibheeshan was infuriatingly unreachable.

'Madam, your Bollywood star will go to jail.'

'What tamasha he did, madam, in the press conference, his wife swearing by her sindoor!' The three men bounded off with the baby-faced man, yelling, 'Saala maadarchod, hang him, madam.' I winced.

'Hey, let's start, Laila, it will become crowded soon.' Vibheeshan appeared suddenly, his cheek glued to his mobile. 'My friend on phone, thoda dost ka call hai,' he said coyly.

'Vibheeshan, where are you, ya? You are supposed to be with me. Your personal calls can be done later, right?'

'Hey, I thought you were just reccing,' he shot back. 'I was attending an important call. Chalo baba, I am ready if *you* are!'

'Let's start… 3—2—1… *cue*…'

'*Not* in his wildest dreams would Bollywood star Upendra ever have imagined that his actions…' I started.

'*Cut*,' the cameraman interrupted.

'Please move out of the frame,' Vibheeshan growled at a curious onlooker who had stepped into his frame. 'Start again,' he ordered.

'*Not* in his wildest dreams would rising Bollywood star, and this year's recipient of best debuting actor from the Starplanet awards, Upendra, have imagined that his actions,' I paused, 'would bring him to such a dark moment in his life.'

'You want to repeat that?' Vibheeshan said.

'Why? What's the issue?' I asked.

'You stopped.'

'Baba, that pause was for effect!'

'Aisa nahi laga, didn't look like a natural pause to me, more like a stumble—this will not work in news. It's too filmy,' Vibheeshan commented.

'Yaar, Vibheeshan, please let me decide. Just because I am from the entertainment beat, everyone is suddenly an expert, giving the Barbie from Bollywood their gyaan on serious news reporting!'

'I am just saying, hum toh sirf cameraman hai, bhaiyya,' Vibheeshan muttered morosely.

'Okay, and can you please get that court banner?'

'I know, I have twelve years of experience,' Vibheeshan muttered and clammed up.

What a cry baby! Indian men are still not used to women giving them orders. Well, I quit being a little girl way back, and so should you, I wished I could shout, but I did not want our little battle to attract any attention.

Surprisingly, as a peace offering, Vibheeshan offered to take the tape from me to the OB van to get the footage uplinked. The OB van was parked a good kilometre away on the other side of the court and in the humid weather I could not ask for more.

'Sure, thanks. Say hi to Mayuri on my behalf.' Vibheeshan blushed at the name of his girlfriend, X Channel's OB engineer. After all, I had to make sure he knew I knew the reason for his sudden generosity.

Upendra had raped his domestic help, nineteen-year-old Julian. Everyone in Bollywood was shocked—one of their kind caught in the act!

Gay activists bayed for his blood. NGOs started signature campaigns. Poor Upsee, a theatre graduate, was even getting the right awards. He was not a bad actor—some would even call him talented. But unfortunately for him, he wasn't well-connected, or maybe he just did not have what it took to be a *star*. And then there were countless conjectures on his sexual orientation. All out in the open now. Upendra called it mutual consent. The grapevine was that Upsee had entered into a sexual relationship with the boy by promising him an introduction to Bollywood's high and mighty producers and agents. But when he didn't keep his word, his manservant turned against him. He claimed to have 'evidence'. Poor Upsee.

He began by denying the charges, even swore on his wife's

head. He then said he was drunk. After that it was mutual consent. I felt bad for his poor wife. What compulsions had made her stand by him?

The help, Julian, had meanwhile got himself a PR agent after countless demands to appear on TV and on gay shows and rights panels. He also had offers pouring in from reality shows. Upendra had finally delivered to Julian what he had promised, only not quite the way either of them had expected.

But for Upendra, it was time for retribution. I could hardly see him at first. He was with his wife. I recognized her chignon. She had dressed down for the occasion—short kurta with plain chikan work and jeans. Her eyes were hidden behind huge dark glasses. Upendra's eyes were bloodshot. He had a dazed expression and snapped when one of the cameramen, Rajesh, got too close to him.

'Careful, Upsee bastard. You don't want more trouble. You have already blown a big fat hole in your own career!' Rajesh muttered.

Upendra was just about to sign the biggest film of his career. Why did he do what he did? Words like consensual sex and scheming servant and conspiracy were thrown in. Julian had gone to town showing the scratches on his back—twenty-two in all, fourteen on the upper back, the rest on the lower back and some on the hip, leaving little to the imagination. He shuttled from one channel to another. The TV channels ranted about how it looked as if an animal had attacked the poor boy, discussions were held on how even men were not safe in the industry, and could a sex-starved maniac be allowed to get away? The verdict was out even before the judge had made up his mind. Poor Upsee never stood a chance. His wife stood with him, holding his hand through every press conference. After a short hearing came a shorter judgement.

'Jail ho gayee,' someone hollered. 'Seven years!'

Everyone started shouting at once. Reporters barking on their phones scrambled to their spots and called the PCRs so that they could go live *first*, breathlessly vomiting out the details. Vibheeshan was ready to go. I had already been wired, my cordless mike lapel in place, the talkback checked, the lip gloss dabbed and the PCR on standby.

In the din I could just about make out my cue.

'And we are joined by Laila who is at… the court premises right now…' A few words of the anchor were lost.

Oh god, did she say cue, I did not hear cue. *Did she say cue?*

And I was on air in seconds.

'*And* judgment day is finally here for Bollywood star Upendra. *Guilty*, the judge said.'

I had to scream over the din to make myself heard in the OB. I was being pushed from all sides. Vibheeshan was nervous about his camera getting knocked down.

The OB continued.

'Hey, hurry up,' someone hissed.

'Break it up, break it up,' someone yelled.

'Don't stop, don't stop,' screamed the PCR in my ear.

'Even we have to do, ya.'

'Achha tamasha laga ke rakha hai.'

'Laila, *go on—do not stop*—continue!' screamed the PCR. 'We need to stay on this! Keep talking, we are rolling shots.'

I was sore, bruised from all the pushing and jostling.

Reporters and cameramen from other channels were yelling at the same time.

English news reporters:

'Upendra's wife was crying.'

'Upendra's wife was howling.'

'Upendra's wife was inconsolable.'

Hindi news reporters:

'Upsee, tumne paap kiya.'

'Uski aankhein laal thee.'

'Woh phoot phoot kar ro raha tha.'

'Uska pati aaj mujrim hai.'

The court premises erupted in an ear-shattering din when he stumbled out of court. Wearing a dazed expression, he held onto his wife tightly. The mikes that were being thrust in his face were pushed aside. Upendra's composure finally cracked and he started sobbing. Cameramen elbowing each other for the best position yelled:

'He is crying, ro raha hai—get that, get that.'

'I want a close-up of his face.'

'Get his expressions, get the wife crying.'

'Get his eyes close up, his fingers, man. What shots!'

Security guards materialized from nowhere, and within seconds Upendra had disappeared from the building along with his posse of security men and friends.

'Expression pakda?' I askedVibheeshan.

'Got side shot only.'

'You didn't? What do you mean, Vibheeshan, you did *not* frigging get it? What the *hell* will I show?' I screeched.

'Bugger moved too fast, motherfucker shoved me! I will

get you a dump, okay!' Vibheeshan shot back and got busy dumping footage on my mini-DVC.

'But I can't understand why you didn't get his front shot.'

'Arrey, I will get you a dump from some other channel ya, chill, okay! Oye, Mayuri, naya tattoo hai kya? Verry nice, haan.' Vibheeshan had obviously found something of greater import to discuss with Mayuri.

'Ya, got it done yesterday,' Mayuri, his girlfriend, gushed as she showed off a fire-breathing dragon tattoo on her neck.

'Check the tracks and audio!' I said to no one in particular.

It was over as quickly as it had started. The wires were pulled out and coiled into neat buns to disappear into the dark confines of the OB vans... sated, emptied. The feed was sent.

'Meet me tonight at eight in my room.' Bunny's curt phone call left me wondering what I had done this time. She sounded hopping mad.

Bitchy is Sexy

'How many times, Laila? Just how many times do I have to save your arse?' Bunny Chopra—razor-sharp editor, devil-incarnate-turned-desk-inquisitor, the alpha beta omega of all bitchy bosses, the mistress of my moments—was going ballistic. The diamond piercing on her chin glinted in unison with the bigger one mounted on her right eyebrow. Outside Bunny's glass cabin, Indu and Lattoo pretended to do their work.

'But Bunny…' I pleaded.

'Just shut up and listen. It's not the first time. Do you know your cameraman has complained to his department head? This is the nth cameraman complaint against you!'

'But Bunny, did you see the footage? The tracks were totally shot! Even the servos wouldn't align them, Bunny,' I shot back. 'Thank god I was carrying an extra tape for dumps.'

'So what? It can happen to anyone. These are machines, for god's sake; it does not give you the right to be rude to the cameraman. Why do you like to fuck their happiness?' Bunny shook her gem-studded index finger at me, her huge kohl-circled eyes ready to pop out. But that had more to do with an ongoing thyroid problem.

'For god's sake, what exactly did he say in the complaint against me?'

'What did you say to Vibheeshan?'

Shit, I thought as Indu and Latika were joined by Nandu, all three of them peering in through the glass cabin's walls, not even pretending to do their work now.

'Me, what did I say? We had a little tiff but it was small; he was stalling the shoot to attend to personal calls—that affair he is having with Mayuri,' I said.

'Well, that's none of your business. Just because you don't have a life. He found you offensive. The camera head has complained. He is threatening to send a written complaint.'

'What a shit,' I swore.

'Laila, I can't do this every time—what was that choot story of yours? Do you know your story on superstar Raaja Babu had to be pulled out—H. Raami was so pissed,' Bunny yelled.

Harindranath Raami, the CEO of EMTV, or H. Raami as he was popularly known, had been sourced from an MNC dealing in investments in developing economies. His limited TV exposure notwithstanding, his qualifications in dealing with Chinese, Latinos and East Africans had impressed the gutkha king enough to appoint him the CEO of a national news channel. But that was not our business, right? One thing was clear: heads rolled when H. Raami was angry.

'So is this about the fight with Vibheeshan or about the

Raaja story?' I suspected the outburst had more to do with the latter. 'There was nothing wrong with my story—if that Bollywood star endorses a particular brand of satellite TV but brazenly installs the rival one at his own house, what's wrong if I make a story?'

'Shut the fuck up, Laila. The channel's satellite providers have threatened blackout of our channel. Your story showed them in poor light—and don't give me that look—as it is, boss is furious at the number of show cause notices the Ministry of Broadcasting is sending for your show. It has too many tits and butt shots. You need to warn your online editor.' Bunny was so agitated by now that her pallu had dropped, revealing her ample bosom.

'But you said it's okay to use sexy shots. You said it's okay to be irreverent,' I said.

'Yeah, but not with some fucking superstar who can send a single SMS to the guy who gives tera-mera salary and fuck our combined happiness. Unless you want to pound masalas for the rest of your pathetic life in gutkha king's factory?'

Bunny had worked her way up from a lowly production assistant who rolled tapes, and made it to editor after a trillion 'sacrifices'. Her most quoted line was: 'Sluts, you know I was called in to work on the day of my grandmother's death. I was rolling a show when my mausi had a heart attack. So don't give me fuck about your dog dying!' It was an open secret that Bunny had an eye on getting a key portfolio in the new entertainment channel—and was trying to cosy up to the bosses in every way possible. And hell awaited anyone who made her look stupid.

People in EMTV said a lot of things about Bunny. The one thing I could vouch for was that she made reporters shed romantic notions in a jiffy. She loved nothing better than abusing hacks to their faces. She loved to be feared. And she had pet hates. For some reason she had put me in the doghouse. I like to think that she wanted to make me tougher.

There was more to come.

'And I must say, your fashion sense is getting from bad to worse. I am sure we pay you enough to buy some decent clothes—Nandu, please take this poor girl to one of your friends, yaar.' Outside, Nandu did not budge. There was no stopping Bunny now.

'Madam, I was reading your fashion-week script. We don't give opinions in this channel, puhleeze go beyond your gyaani reportage. Do not get metaphorical and arty-farty on me. This is entertainment. Don't be too ambitious, thank you! Quite frankly, you better shape up, there are fifty girls ready to take your job, girl.'

'Huh,' I croaked.

But I almost got molested at the Lizard Lounge at South Extension while hosting *Filmy Masti*.

But I almost came to blows with the sloshed manager who insisted on coming into the frame each time I went live.

But after wrapping up from office at 2 a.m. I was at the courts at eleven the next morning for Upendra's hearing…

Did I have the guts to say any of this to Bunny? Hah and *hah*!

I did not want to jeopardize my chances of going to Amsterdam for the IIFA; I had been left out for three years and if I kept the editor happy long enough, she had assured me the trip was mine this time.

'Do you think you can cover Fardeen's party at O-Lounge tonight without a catastrophe?' she continued. 'Sweetie,' she beseeched Nandu, our in-house star, 'please see madam's script and whip it up into something airable… only you can do it!'

Choke, gulp, don't scream, swallow it, it's just an insult. Good thing I had learned to cultivate an obtuse-too-dumb-to-understand-she-is-being-insulted expression. It took away the sting of public humiliation. It was just another night at the coveted entertainment desk in the most coveted English news channel.

Suddenly covering manholes and installing nullahs did not seem such a bad idea after all.

Status: Standby

'That's just it! You are being so bloody unfair. You of all people think I am getting away with something,' I yelled at Rehan when I finally reached our two-bedroom apartment in Vasant Enclave. It was a joint investment, which ate into 70 per cent of our joint savings but remained empty for eighteen hours a day. 'You don't realize I work very hard!'

'S-stop being so aggro… I just wanted you to be there for the party. Dad was asking about y-you,' Rehan stammered. As he always did when we had an altercation. Rehan, my boyfriend from college days. People said he was quite a catch with his model-type good looks and a steady job. Rehan had a sharp sense of humour, and with his vulnerable eyes and boyish pale face, he could be very sexy.

And so many years later, nothing had changed. Or at least nothing seemed to have changed.

Rehan made me feel like the sexiest person in the world. I loved his guts, his quick wit. He loved what he called my restless energy. He had left his cushy family business to become a management trainee in an international bank, then he left that job and invested all his savings in studying an advanced Master's in management of global enterprises with a focus on developing economies.

Rehan was the first person I had run to screaming with happiness when I landed the EMTV job, long before I told papa and ma. We moved in together soon after.

And now, after one-and-a-half years of living together, Rehan wanted to take our relationship to the next level. I should have been happy, right? But I was scared shitless. Shaadi-waadi today? Kids-wids tomorrow? No frigging way.

'But I am not in a comfortable position right now… Bunny will…'

'No, Laila! That's just it! Your life revolves around pleasing Bunny. She has you on a leash, and a pretty short one at that! You *used* to love reporting, but now I think you are only driven by this fear of failing in *her* eyes!' Rehan's soft voice became hard. He could be assertive when he wanted something—but I thought he was being uncharacteristically pig-headed.

'Every time Bunny calls, you jump like an automaton. You are not her slave. For the last two months, every day you have reached home after 2 a.m., you disappear in the morning—I don't even feel like we are living together any more. Just because you lost out on the IIFA thing last time, you were depressed for days; have you seen yourself lately? You don't even smile any more when you go to work!'

'Just try living one fucking day of my fucking life—you will not last one shift!' I was close to tears. 'It's my dream job, Rehan! There are fifty girls dying to take my job. If I blow it, if I don't get the numbers, Bunny will have my arse.'

'Laila, she would not have given the show to you if she thought you would blow it.'

'I should have let Lattoo do this show. She is so pretty she won't even need a script. Men will pay just to watch her standing like a statue—'

'Last time I checked it was news, not fashion TV, Laila.'

'You have no idea about TV.'

'Laila, I know you are working hard, but all I am saying is that this time I wanted you to meet my family. *We* have a life too. Or at least we did.'

'Listen, I am sorry—okay, I overreacted but… but it's just these couple of months before my yearly assessment review report—I think I am getting there! Bunny has been hinting at the ESOPs and the company car, you know… it will help both of us,' I said.

'It will help you. I am fine with you even now.'

'Chop, chop. So what did Tootsie say about me now?' Tootsie was my nickname for Rehan's mother on account of her rather formidable buck teeth.

'Mummy hates the name of your show, *Raat Rani*. She thinks it sounds trashy,' Rehan teased.

'For god's sake, *Raat Rani* is not my show. Mine is *Filmy Masti*! Anyway, who asked for Tootsie's opinion?'

Rehan's mother made this weird face and her eyes got a mean look whenever she saw me around her son. I thought it was probably because she thought I was not good enough for him. I disliked her. But this was because she hardly ever made me feel welcome. I was just returning the favour.

'What about your dad?' he said, ignoring my response.

Shit. Why did he have to ask? I felt my stomach go all queasy.

'I guess he is okay,' I mumbled.

'Why guess? Why don't you call him?'

'And have a shouting match?'

'Just talk to him!'

'Talk about *what*, Rehan? Because he does not let me speak. I know he does not like what I do but why can't he be happy for me? Last time I spoke to him he asked me to change my beat! He said, why don't I do business stories! He wants me to do nice decent environment stories like that nice decent reporter he saw on TV—it is bloody frustrating!'

'He is concerned.'

'Papa is concerned that I am not yet married. He calls you to confirm that *you* are still with me, not whether *I* am still with you!'

'What's the difference? In any case, why don't we get married then?'

'Man, are you serious? I have… like…'

'Ya, ya, you have to worry about your ESOPs and your company car, and pleasing Bunny, and of course, let's not forget meeting your stars, but seriously, let's call your dad—wait, did you call him?'

'Why should he miss out on all the fun, haan?' I said.

'Shut up.'

'What did he say?'

'Shut up, dude.'

'C'mon. Vent.'

'I said I have a new show. He said stop this tamasha and get married if you have to do this sort of thing. Then do whatever you want. He did not even listen to what I had to say. Man, I am feeling so violent now.'

My relationship with papa, to put it mildly, was a lot more complicated. He criticized my choices in life, my TV career, my reporting beat, my living-in with Rehan, so much that he ended up alienating me. And as I said, I am good at returning the favour. Rehan had even tried to hide from me the fact that papa had done a background check on him and was so pleased with Rehan's economics background that he had suggested to Rehan's father that it was high time we got hitched if we had to continue with this sort of thing.

I did not have it in me to get into that space today. Neither did Rehan.

Sex it Up

❧

So tell me again why I joined TV?

On EMTV, chief political correspondent and superstar anchor Rene Chaddha was breaking the news—
'Terrorists stormed into one of Afghanistan's largest military air bases, Bagram air base, killing at least ten people… Terrorists have managed to destroy two US-supplied advanced surveillance aircraft, P-3C Orion planes…'

In the cold make-up room, I waited patiently for my turn to puff up, as some big boys from prime-time news got their eyebrows done. There were just three chairs and all three were taken. But I could wait. News came first, even for a puff job.

'You know *she* told me to hide the fact that there are UN officials in my VT—she wants to break it herself—*according to reports just received and we are breaking it on EMTV by super-fuckin'- star-Rene Chadhha,'* Antim, a pasty-faced newbie news anchor-cum-producer, vented to an important prime-time news anchor while getting his face scrubbed clean. Rene was reading her link into breaking news on the make-up room TV.

'*They entered the high-security Bagram air base in Kabul. They set off eight huge explosions in a space of thirty minutes... the terrorists' first targets were aircraft parked on the tarmac and equipment in the nearby hangars; the siege continues as we speak. For more, I am joined by Omar Naseerullah Babbar, correspondent, Islamabad Times.*'

'Shit! God, can't they get anything right! It's associate editor, not correspondent. Get me the PCR.'

Antim hollered on the phone at someone in the PCR, 'Please change the name of the super, it's wrong! Check my VT published on-edit-7a.m.!' He banged down the phone. 'You know, I did that phono. I tracked Naseerullah Babbar—I had to teach that dumb cunt how to pronounce his name—I got his numbers, asked the questions, wrote the VT and handed it over to madam superstar Rene Chaddha; bloody hot-shot bitch does not even bother to check the supers, ya!'

Shit, that reminds me, I have to change my supers—I called Chiki to change the headers.

'No. Just write, "Ranbir's New Item Number", the second header is "Salman ki Masti", the third can be "Katrina Wants a National Award Instituted for Item Numbers".'

'Wow! Such enthusiasm for tinsel town in the morning.' Antim looked at me and laughed.

'Hero ki *masti*, heroine *sasti*—what fun! I wish our lives were this fun,' the prime-time news anchor snorted. And then both of them started guffawing.

Behenchods. I could not believe these guys. Their arses were on fire but they thought, no, believed, that they were entitled to free manoranjan!

'I see your eyebrows are done, laydeez. How pretty they look!' I said snidely. 'Now you can update the latest death count in Bagram air base. Thirty-six people dead now. By the way, how was the hair spa at Martina's?'

And left.

As I said, it had started as the perfect day. Nothing could possibly go wrong. I had a fantastic line up in the show's run order. Shah Rukh's party followed by Salman on his love life, fantastic shots of Katrina at the Ajmer Sharif dargah, and an exclusive photo shoot with Kareena. I even had a Sunny Leone chat. She was planning to leave hardcore porn and I was sure the viewers would be pucca interested in her reasons for leaving. I loved days like this. The VTs were edited on time, the tickers were on air, the donut was ready, the supers were in. Even the PCR was calm and happy.

It happened after the second story. I was into my third link. Normally, I make it a point to memorize my links by heart, but today, as I said, nothing should have gone wrong. Well, it did. The teleprompter collapsed right in the middle of the third link. There I stood, staring at the black camera lens, struck dumb. I couldn't remember what to say. I cannot ever forget the shape of that black lens in that terrifying moment of complete public mortification, resembling a black hole into which I fervently wished I would disappear. The Columbus had become corrupt and the channel was about to hit 'black'

(hitting black is right up there in the list of worst production glitches, but that's not my fault!).

The producer was yelling in my ears to ad-lib (translate: Keep talking till we have something to put on air).

'About what?' I wanted to yell back. But I couldn't. I was on air.

'Laila!' the producer hollered maniacally into my earpiece. 'Just faff about something, some gossip... kuch toh bolo, any masala about some actor, ya! For heaven's sake, you are a Bolly hack, dude!'

But I didn't. I couldn't. The moments stretched to an eternal minute—actually, the longest forty-six seconds of my life. They finally crashed to an ad. By then my mortification was complete. A small technical kink had reduced me from an all-knowing show anchor to a complete jerk.

Word travelled fast.

'Hey, what happened with you in the PCR today during your anchoring?' Indu asked loudly. 'I heard there was quite a tamasha!' Shit. Nothing escaped Indu, who still hadn't got over the fact that I had got my own daily show before her and missed no opportunity to rub it in. Her screech pierced Bunny's cabin.

'Lail-aa! Did you screw up today?' Bunny hollered from her cabin.

'Umm, yes, Bunny. It was not my fault though.'

Shit. Everyone was at the desk. I wanted to disappear into my cubicle. I slumped down in my chair, hoping the bulky screen would hide my face sufficiently.

'Puhleeze spare me the sordid details! Columbus *fails*. Deal

with it. Why the fuck didn't you just gossip about some actor?'
Bunny said.

'Babe, you will never make a TRP reporter,' Nandu shook
his head. He always accused me of being too concerned with the
angle and not the entertainment. Nandu said I had no connect
with the masses, no masala in my stories, so they were often
relegated to the last segment of my own entertainment show.

'The people want tamasha, not the truth,' Nandu enlightened
me for the nth time. 'No one would have noticed if you had just
gone on and on about Sonam wearing butt pads at Cannes, or
Bipasha and John's breakup, or Minissha's nose job. You know,
I was with H. Raami last night and even he said we need to be
more irreverent!'

'But how come? Was there a meeting with him? I did not
know!' I said anxiously.

'He called me to his farmhouse party. What power play—all
the big daddies, editors, filmstars... arrey, Latika was there too,
she danced scandalously with that actor in Shyamu Sharma's
film. Hey, I did not see you, where were you? You did not
come,' Nandu asked.

'No, I was at the Fardeen party in Gurgaon. Bunny told me
to cover it.' I tried to keep the disappointment out of my voice.

'How mean! Poor kid! You work so much, na,' interrupted
Indu, her cold fingers patting my burning cheeks.

'What a bitch party! Gentlemen and girls, I am dead!' All
heads turned at Latika's husky purring. She could make a
hangover look sexy.

'Tired after dirty dancing? That was quite a show you put
up last night, sweetie!' Indu said.

'You liked? Thanks. Was I good?'

Sarcasm was lost on Latika.

'But where were you after you disappeared with the actor?'

'Which actor? Oh, that little boy! What rubbish, he was such a cheyyp—I just wanted to talk to Shyamu, ya. He is really fascinating, this film he is working on, he wants to do an underbelly of Bollywood type film.' Latika seemed strangely animated. 'I am going for a smoke, you wanna come?' she drawled and walked out without a second glance at us.

'Grreeat! She wafts in at 4.45 p.m. and floats out at 4.51 p.m.! Madam Lattoo has broken her own record of straight seven minutes at the desk.' Indu said it loud enough, hoping that Bunny would hear.

'You wait and see, in three years we will be covering her events. Have you seen the way directors look at her? She will get a part in some Bollywood film, become a heroine and then you can publish stories on her!' Chiki shot back at Indu. It was not like Chiki was Lattoo's knight in shining armour or something, but Chiki hated Indu. And the feeling was mutual. Chiki had once intercepted an abusive email concerning her that Indu had been tossing around. Their catfight could be heard two floors up and Bunny had to cut short an important meeting with the bosses to intervene. Both had to issue a public apology and were let off with stern warnings. Since then, Indu and Chiki being in the same vicinity always led to trouble.

'Nandu, your foreign exchange is here!' Sunny Singh from production control hollered.

'You going abroad? You did not tell me? Where?' I asked.

'Okay, Sunny!' Nandu called out. He turned to me. 'Arrey, just a junket.'

'Nandu, stop being so secretive. Guess what! Bunny has promised that I will be going to IIFA this time,' I said. 'Nands, I am so excited—you must tell me what you want from there.'

'Laila, I am going to Amsterdam—for IIFA, sweetie.'

'Nice try, Nandu!' I said disbelievingly.

'Sorry, Laila. Nandu is going for IIFA,' Bunny interrupted. 'I hope that's okay with you, ma'am!'

'No problem! But I thought you had promised me,' I said, trying my best not to sound whiny.

'I am not here to hand out favours, babe! Nandu will get twenty masala stories from there in a day, and you?'

'But you know I can get the stuff too.'

'This conversation is over, sweetie,' Bunny dismissed me. 'Just write that Bollywood masala and show it to Nandu—he will spice it up. But you can do the Ronsher Khanna presser. If you want to be taken seriously, get me sexy headers for tomorrow.' Bunny definitely had a way about her. Of course, no one would call her endearing.

In a TV news organization, a thick-skinned bloody fool always has a better shot at life. I thought I was a bit of both. I was confident that I stood a better chance at being a reporter. Nandu disagreed. He felt I had to be more of a nautanki wali. He said my problem was that at the core, I still considered journalism an honourable profession. But the mask was slipping and the romantic fibs were over. I was coming to terms with the reality of my career. There were consumers for all sorts of entertainment goodies. The fickle audience changed its loyalties on a whim. It better be solid tamasha. Or they wanted their money back.

From Shah Rukh's brawl at Wankhede Stadium to *Dabangg*'s golden girl taking a tumble on the ramp; from Akshay Kumar posing next to ailing cartoonist R.K. Laxman's bed in the hospital to getting his wife to publicly zip up his trousers; papa Bachchan telling editors how to do their job and warning the media to quit messing with his son's career to Salman Khan's cocky behaviour or the unfortunate Vivek Oberoi's infamous press conference where he took on Salman Khan; John's briefs to Bipasha's *Jism*; SRK's six packs to Katrina's lip job; Deepika's ill-fated tattoo to the Shahid-Kareena breakup; Govinda slapping a fan to Shobhaa Dé being called a 'menopausal old hag' by a bunch of prissy little industry boys whose male egos she hurt… the list was endless.

'Baby, we are not running *Krishi Darshan* here! We have to get sexy stories,' Nandu said.

'These glamorous stars are not your friends. As far as they are concerned, you are just the help. So you are allowed to arsewhip most of them most of the time,' chimed in Chiki. God, stupid punk.

'What about the ramifications?' I was dumb enough to ask.

'Simple. *Don't* get caught, stupid,' Nandu said.

'Sweetie, no point looking for impractical virtues or three quarters of TV news will be deleted instantly, for being no more than Chinese whispers!' Bunny shot back.

Please note: The general premise of the stories that were considered sexy in entertainment seemed to spin around someone's utter humiliation. Bitchy is sexy.

Smart reporting included off-the-cuff remarks from people who would not identify themselves—from a source close to the star/a member of the film crew—please note, not the make-up artist said, not the choreographer said, but some ephemeral source who cannot be named or pinned down.

So what stops a hack from concocting a totally fictitious story by quoting sources who need not be named to verify her unverifiable story? Nothing. And do they even give a damn about the truth? As famous American journalist Martha Gellhorn said, 'Journalism and truth... balls, balls, balls.'

No Show

He was late. Hours late. But who did you complain to? He was not a chhota-mota star, he was Ronsher Khanna, the *enfant terrible* of Bollywood. The flustered PR agents seemed increasingly clueless about Ronsher's whereabouts. The Bollywood superstar had left his emperor-sized, super-deluxe, madly expensive suite in one of the most expensive hotels in New Delhi a good four hours earlier, with a promise to return in forty-five minutes. But Ronny was playing hookie. The minutes had turned into painful hours, and there was still no sign of him. The PR folks had another problem in their hands: the belligerent media was in no mood to be placated.

'How can you guys treat us like this?' screeched Saryu, an acclaimed author of entirely fictitious stories and grossly caricatured facts, who did *whatever* it took to get that byte. She was highly prized by her channel and had made it from reporter to special correspondent within a year.

'This is soo unprofessional,' Mridul, known for her hysterical reportage, wailed.

'But where is Ronny? How long do we wait?' someone asked.

'You know, we should stage a walkout,' Saryu shrieked for the third time. What Saryu lacked in height she more than made up for in the vocals department. Pint-sized Saryu's irritating high-pitched screech always got recorded in every channel's microphone.

'Saala… I can't wait any more!'

'Then go, na. All bijli, no barish, eh Saryu,' teased Manoj, a senior print photographer with a national daily.

'Fuck you,' Saryu snapped.

'With pleasure,' said Manoj.

'Guys, please take this someplace else,' Gogol, still busy working on his book during shoots, looked up from his laptop, annoyed as hell at having his chain of thought interrupted. Gogol, thin as a matchstick and sharp as a razor, was the only one who was not angry with Ronny for being late—but the noisy altercation had made him mad. 'Can't we be civilized, ya? Why are you behaving like junglees? Just take your issues someplace else.'

'And you are busy doing?' Saryu raised her eyebrows.

'I promise I will tell you someday, sweetie,' shot back Gogol, 'when you grow up!'

Someone whistled.

I had arrived a good couple of hours after the time printed on the invite. I walked in on a posse of sweating and sulking TV reporters—they had been waiting in the press room of the hotel for three hours.

'We should teach them a lesson!' screeched Saryu in her whiniest voice.

'Why do we give these actors so much bhaav?'

'Excuse me! Who… who called him an actor?'

'Well,' a nervous Ritika tried to reassure us, 'he gave a monster hit.'

'Inkey peechhe marte ho tabhi daudaatey hai,' hissed Saryu.

'But where is Ronsher… it's been four hours,' Minal said irritably.

'Wasn't he at Kingdom of Dreams last night? Wahin kahin so gaya hoga,' someone mocked.

'Arrey, this is too much… hadd ho gayi, yaar!'

'Ronsher ne di googly! I think I will make a story on this.'

'We should walk out now. His stupid PR people are clueless. They can't confirm whether he is coming at all.'

'Ya-ya-ya, let's go now, man… teach him a lesson!'

Of course, no one made any attempt to move. Each reporter was waiting for the other to make the first move. They were all bluffing. The truth was that most of them would bully, flatter, lie, bust a gut, break a leg rather than abandon this particular star quarry. Several arrests for drunken driving, assaulting with intention to harm not proven, outrageous unprovoked and sometimes provoked attacks on photographers, public and private run-ins with co-stars, and unlawful possession of firearms—his huge list of misdemeanours had only increased Ronsher's glamour. With Ronsher Khanna, it was always a big fat news day.

Simple arithmetic: one Ronsher equalled three headlines, four VTs and five bizarre quotes.

'It's the way the guy is wired.'
'Look at the way he walks and glares.'
'He is a bhandaar of stories.'
'I will get my three-day quota!'

He is here. Someone announced Ronsher's arrival and all hell broke loose.

'Behenchod neeche chala gaya hai.'
'Hey, you crack, you hit me.'
'Arrey, lift ke paas best bet.'
'Did you see how that schmuck pushed me!'
'Madam, aap saamne se hatiye.'
'You idiot, you broke my strap.'
'Fatty has blocked my way.'
'What a nuisance.'
'What a jerk.'
'What's going on!'

Suddenly there was a shortage of security to handle the uncontrollable media. The celebrity riot hit the hotel lobby. Taking in the mood of the press, Ronsher was escorted by his bouncers into the interior of the plush hotel, now converted into an impregnable fortress.

'Hey, why isn't he coming to the media room?' the press erupted. 'We can't wait any longer.'

The PR lady yelled back with sudden confidence, 'He just needs to freshen up.' She knew the press wasn't going anywhere.

'Chalo, at least he is here, ab jaayega kahan?'

It was only one hour later that Ronsher, eyes swollen and red, finally swaggered in wearing tight jeans and a tighter tee.

'I don't wanna talk to *you*... and *you*!' Ronny drawled petulantly, rolling his eyes, pointing his fingers at two reporters and glaring at their mikes.

It was unexpected but no one was really surprised. You had to expect stuff like this when you were interviewing Ronsher.

What had miffed Ronny? Probably some story he saw on their channels. Couldn't have been complimentary, judging by his black mood.

'Okay, start, who is first?' the superstar barked.

Rahul from News Today started with straight questions. I was second.

I had my brief clear:

a. Let him speak.

b. Get a 'sexy' headline for tomorrow.

Poor Rahul did everything he could. But Ronsher answered peevishly in monosyllables.

It suddenly dawned on me that matters would soon get worse.

The television set that Ronsher was looking at intently was tuned in to my show which was set to start in a couple of minutes. He couldn't have missed the 'Don't miss *Ronsher ke Raaz* on *Filmy Masti* at 8.30 p.m. today' donut being run repeatedly. It was 8.27 p.m. and the channel was on an ad break.

Three minutes to the big bang. Because...

Because, the problem was, the first three stories on my show were about what a crappy actor Ronsher was. The stories clearly brought out why Ronsher was easily the most hated actor in Bollywood—his on-and-off love life with actresses and models, his boorish run-ins with the media, his arm-twisting his producers. And then the story on Bollywood actors above forty who refused to grow up, with an unflattering focus on *guess who*! And the fourth story was on Ronsher losing not just his girlfriend but also his hairline and his waistline, with lots of shots of the star looking his paunchy and bleary best!

Sensing impending disaster and complete humiliation, I panicked. I looked around desperately, wondering how to stall him, but Rahul had wrapped his interview.

Three seconds to the Big Bang.

Marti kya na karti. I got up and did something I had never done before.

'Hey, Ronsher.' I was at his feet, gushing embarrassingly. 'You fulfilled my dream today, man. Just by being here. I am your biggest fan on the planet and my family loves you. Can I have one photo with you before we start the interview?' It was my most nauseating performance, but at that moment, I didn't care.

Ronsher turned around and fixed me with his stare. A sunny smile split his face. Behind his head my show had started, and the first story read: *Bollywood's Baddest Boy*…

'No sweat, sweetheart,' Ronsher declared magnanimously.

'OMG, look who descended from her stratosphere!' someone smirked loudly.

'Kehti hai I-am-too-good-for-this-autograph business? Ab toh photo chahiye, bhaiyya!'

'Oye, motu. Oye, chubby. Hey, handsome,' Ronny whistled and summoned a fat reporter standing nearby.

'Abbey motu, let's see how good you are behind the camera!' drawled Ronsher in an East London accent which he used when speaking to English channel reporters.

Behind Ronny's head, a story on his shitty fights and eccentric behaviour was being telecast; the video editor had used vivid flashes of lightning and thunder to accentuate Ronny's run-ins with co-stars and media. And bold text in red screaming: *Ronsher's latest tamasha…*

Meanwhile, motu stepped forward to do the job. Ronsher posed for my 'me-with-star pix'. My cameraperson was stumped at my sudden bout of star-sickness. The event manager Neeraj stared bug-eyed, remembering only too well when I had screamed blue murder at unprofessional reporters scraping and fawning at the altar of Bollywood stars.

Manoj muttered, 'How embarrassing!'

Gogol hissed, 'So typical.'

Now the story on the screen was: *Ronsher—unlucky in love…*

I took some more autographs, now for my nephew and niece.

More hisses followed.

'Hey, we need to really get on here,' Gogol said.

'Arrey, what's this?' Saryu asked, annoyed.

Whatever, I thought.

A happy Ronsher is far better than an angry one. My show rolled on in the background. I don't remember the questions, nor the answers. But that's not the point. I survived Ronsher.

I received an SMS from Bunny. The Manali shoot was on with Bollywood actor Amar Kapoor. Also, Indu had just won some broadcasting award for her feature story. *Shit!* She was treating everyone to Chinese. *Great.*

I should have missed the lunch. Lattoo cribbed like crazy. She had still not been put on anchoring and wanted to ditch the job and marry her British boyfriend.

Indu told Lattoo to quit her randi rona. Latika spent the rest of the evening sulking. But Indu was actually more pissed off with Bunny for handing over prime shoots to Nandu. Chiki, meanwhile, was in big trouble because she went off to sleep in the middle of a shoot and created a ruckus when she was woken up. The event manager sent a written complaint about Chiki to Bunny and H. Raami.

Ad Lib

'So, you do weddings?'
'She *covers* weddings.'

'She is a page three reporter.'

'Bollywood, fashion, page three... all the same thing nowadays!'

'Ya, sure, aunty. You name it. Kitty parties. Baby showers. Godbharai. I do everything. You have any in mind?'

Lunch with Rehan's family was potentially explosive. There was a time when I used to freeze and smile sheepishly at every Jack and Jill in Rehan's extended family poking fun at my job. Not any more.

I tried to down some stone-cold spaghetti and chips with lukewarm wine. I hate spaghetti because (a) it sticks to the intestines and (b) it is the most difficult carb to melt. But the lavish affair constituting sour pork, glutinous rice, raw-fish curries and deep-fried pudding made me gag. Across the stately hall of the Sainik Farms mansion, I saw Rehan trying to make his way towards me.

'Can she get Malaika to dance at the shaadi? Or John Abraham, woh toh aa hee jaayega.'

'Shah Rukh would be very expensive, na?'

'Verrrry,' I said.

'What about Katrina?'

'Prrricey,' I said.

'Priyanka?'

'Too busy. You know, I normally charge for these consultations.'

'Laila, there you are,' Rehan butted in as aunty's eyes bulged out.

'How you doing?' Rehan whispered as he dragged me away.

'What do you expect? Your idiotic aunt will probably ask me to do her precious daughter's shaadi shoot. I am sure your mother has told everyone I do shaadi videos,' I hissed back.

'Sweetie, are you enjoying yourself?' Rehan's mother's voice rang out from behind us.

'Yes, yes! Aunty, hi!'

'Night shift?' Rehan's mother inquired as she looked at my choice of apparel for the night, a sequinned tee and jeans, which I thought looked glam without being over the top.

'No, no, just dressing down. Had no time to shop!'

'You are not eating anything? All sticks and bones.' I felt like an uncared-for orphan. 'Try the sour pork.' And with a long look at Rehan, which could have meant n number of things, she swished away.

Fuck.

'She means no harm. Just looking out for me,' Rehan teased.

'Well, excuse me, Rehan. Anyway, I have to leave in twenty.'

'Why? The function is yet to start. Try to spend some time with them. As it is, you are missing the wedding. You are definitely going to Manali to do Amar Kapoor?'

'Pukka.'

'And Nandu is going too?'

'Oh, god. It's not a pleasure trip, in case that's bothering you.'

'But why Nandu? Why not a female reporter?'

'Because he organized it, Rehan. He and Amar Kapoor went to the same school! For god's sake!'

'At least take a female cameraperson. You realize you will be travelling with three men, including Nandu and the cab driver?'

'Thanks for the warning! I am not sneaking off to some rave party! In any case, trust me, compared to this crowd,' I looked around, 'I will be in far safer company!'

Continuity

*I think if there was ever a story worth telling, it would be
whether people have recovered from their childhood or not.*

— ANONYMOUS

I had never seen superstar Amar Kapoor this happy. This
excited. This young. As I rushed to catch up with him on
the long meandering roads of Manali, I knew this was a very
special shoot for the young superstar, who had just given
the biggest hit of his career. Back in his school after ten long
years to inaugurate a new hi-fi gymnasium and boxing rink
to be named after him, he was the guest of honour at the
special commemoration day of his alma mater Rangers.

Nandu, a Rangers' alumni, who had actually pitched the
junket to Bunny, was in the throes of absolute nostalgia. But the
thing is, I hate hill trips. Even trips through midget hills freak
me out. I mean I love the hills, but I am just not built for long
car journeys through the hills. I have always been made to feel
bad about my hillphobia. On the days I have had to undertake

long car journeys, my brains ossify, my limbs go on mass leave, the senses shut down and my stomach revolts big time.

Packing energy food was priority number one. I went with extra spicy Monaco crispies, gallons of Brute's energy drink, rum-based chocolates to deaden my senses, and very sour lime candies to curb the urge to vomit. Vomit bags, a quick change of tees and some lime-based air freshener, excellent in annihilating vomit smells, were also part of the package.

It was a foggy winter morning in Delhi. I trudged to the car with my heavy equipment and tapes. Nandu stopped for a quick smoke. We had an unexpected co-passenger. Chiki had hopped in for a free ride to meet her 'idol' Amar Kapoor. While I had no objection to the lady's impromptu desire to meet Kapoor, it botched up my plans for a comfortable ride. Of course, Rehan was very pleased with the Chiki development. At least now I was not travelling alone with two men.

'Hi, Chiki, you coming with us?' I asked.

'Yeah, duh! Till death do us part, sweetie. (Please note: no *can I*, *may I*, just *ya, deal with it*.) I don't think Laila here is pleased that I am coming,' Chiki complained loudly to Nandu. Outspoken and brazen, Chiki made me feel like an intruder on my own trip. But when she took out a fag to share with Nandu I knew I had better shut up. Smokers form a bond far deeper than any on the esoteric level. I did not stand a chance.

So three journalists were stuffed into the back seat of an Innova. I grabbed the window seat, determined not to be bothered by the smoke. It was going to be a long ride. Kapoor was to join us at some midpoint near Simsa village, four kilometres away from our final destination, Manali's scenic

Kanyal hills, which housed Rangers. Nandu and I would hop into Kapoor's car, after which I was supposed to do my Hindi p-to-c with the actor in the background. I had major misgivings about the whole shoot, as making Bollywood actors speak in Hindi, let alone hold protracted conversations, was an uphill task. There was an unfathomable reluctance amongst most Hindi film actors to talk to the media in their mother tongue. The thought that I would have to make Kapoor, who was not exactly known for his patience, do something he may not want to do made me nervous.

It was a gruelling ride, and I was exhausted. I felt unkempt and dirty. I was in no form to conduct an interview with a Bollywood star. Even the radiant sunlight now spreading across the mystical Kanyal hills failed to lift my sagging spirits. Curiously, Nandu and Chiki, both Delhiites, seemed unaffected by the drive, making me feel worse.

'Oh! Balls.' I covered my face with my silk scarf, which had been doused liberally with mood alleviating fragrances.

Chiki tittered. 'Oh, look at her… Laila is eating her scarf!'

'Ha, ha and ha, Chiki,' I retorted peevishly.

'Girl! Stop being so grumpy.' Nandu punched me affectionately.

'Na, baba, I am just trying not to vomit,' I replied.

'She is getting her beauty sleep,' Chiki butted in. 'Laila wants to bowl Kapoor over with her gorgeous looks!'

I hate it when I can't come up with clever repartees, but I was exhausted so I let it pass.

⚜

Dhabas zipped by, but we had decided to ignore our hunger pangs and go full throttle. I took out some munchies and offered them around but it seemed that smoke and boisterous gossip was all the fuel the two of them needed. Shit. I wish I were as uber-cool. I was feeling totally neglected. I made some half-hearted attempts at small talk but managed to arouse zero interest, so I gave up and continued with my gloomy state of detachment.

As I took out my mirror, a pasty face stared back at me. Nothing that a dab of Mac powder base and strawberry lip gloss could not fix, if only the hilly roads would stop shaking our car by its neck.

Chiki smiled secretively as she texted something of great importance to someone. Nandu smoked away with a faraway look in his eyes, as his alma mater approached. Finally we stopped at a peaceful stretch when the light seemed perfect for our p-to-cs.

'A very different journey for Amar Kapoor who returns to school as chief guest to inaugurate his school's new boxing rink and high-tech gymnasium.'

I practised saying it in Hindi.

We were intercepted by Amar Kapoor's car at Simsa village. The jumbo SUV seemed to stretch itself to cover Kapoor's hulking frame. He was followed by his nineteen-year-old girlfriend, the lithe and toothy young badminton-player-turned-actress Poorva Babi. Outside it had started to rain.

Nandu had a head start with Kapoor. Though separated by generations, they inhabited their own school world. An outsider, I had precious little to contribute to their school-was-heaven conversation. My own school life, spent in an Anglo-Indian institution in Delhi, with strict teachers indiscriminately handing out corporal punishment, was ghastly. Claims to rose-tinted school memories never cut ice with me.

'What's it like returning on the same road you travelled?' Nandu asked.

'Actually, it's very different but feels good. I'm happy to be back in Rangers. I love this place, the atmosphere, the campus… there is nothing like this in the whole world,' Amar said.

Time for me to get some Hindi bytes.

'Kaisa lag raha hai, coming back after so many years?' I asked Kapoor.

'I just told Nandu,' Amar teased me.

I squirmed. 'Ya. But if you can say the same thing in Hindi.'

'Achha lag raha hai!' He burst out laughing.

'School ki memories?'

'Gidney Hall, the cafeteria, Bateyrr…' he said.

'You remember Bateyrr?' Nandu and Amar exchanged merry notes.

'Ha ha, of course, there was no one like him. Those bulging eyes! You know, he caned me,' Amar Kapoor reminisced about the school where he had spent his childhood. 'I was a pampered child and this place was so hostile and unfriendly in the beginning that I wanted to run away. Imagine, I am back! And as a star!' Amar Kapoor sounded boyishly delighted.

'Superstar. Rockstar.' Poorva Babi smiled indulgently.

'I was such a failure, a dickhead loser in school! Imagine, now I am the chief guest!'

'Hmmm… imagine,' I sighed.

'I was miserable about leaving my parents, especially my mother, who was quite devastated. But they sent me to boarding school so that I could learn some discipline, though it killed them to send me so far away.'

'What are you looking forward to now?'

'Meeting the girls. My class hotties! They must be mummies and aunties by now. *Hot* mummies and aunties!' Kapoor laughed.

'Ha ha. You are so funny, Amar Kapoor. Ha ha. Isn't he such a rockstar?' Poorva giggled.

'I am sure your friends must be looking forward to meeting you,' I said.

'So you are Laila… Are you married?' Amar asked and before I could answer, he continued, 'If you are not, I can fix you up with Pandey here!'

Pandey, Amar Kapoor's old classmate from fifth standard, had kindly offered to drive us. He and Amar whispered something to each other and guffawed.

I felt like an intruder and was at a loss on how to react. What made me more anxious was that Kapoor was not bothering to give a single byte in Hindi. But interrupting him did not seem to be a viable option.

Then I saw a sulking Chiki peering at us through the window in the car trailing us and felt better instantly.

Finally we reached the imposing Rangers school that was anxiously awaiting for its superstar alumnus. Kapoor hopped out of the car and underwent a transformation when he entered the school. The hulk of a man suddenly became a lanky teenager. Vittal, our cameraperson, standing tall at six feet six inches himself, was getting increasingly miffed at being jostled by the mammoth crowd around Kapoor. Kids of all ages were going berserk, their parents fared no better. But Kapoor was enjoying every moment. The first stop in Amar Kapoor's itinerary of the school's old haunts was the boxing rink.

'This is the Barrow boys' boxing rink—hey, that was my locker—you know, I was the king of the ring, a goliath. But I still didn't get a cubicle because I was never a prefect! That hurt a lot. I was never thought good enough to be prefect. Does not matter much today though, haan, Pandey?' Amar said, as old friends and starstruck strangers came up to him and hugged him. 'Laila, do you want a byte here?'

'Yeah, sure.' I was hopeful at once.

'You know, I used to drop pencils here!'

'Excuse me?' Every one of his pals started guffawing.

'Do you know why?' Amar asked me.

'No,' I said, waiting to be enlightened.

'Girls wearing really short skirts would bend down to pick the pencils up. Har, har!' Kapoor's humour found many takers.

'Hmmmph, ha ha. Oh god, you are such a trouper! I can't imagine anyone else with such a wicked sense of humour. Kapoor, I wish I was in your school. I have so many short skirts, you know—ha ha!' Poorva's high-pitched laughter was infectious. Appropriate or not, I could not help joining in.

As the sun dipped behind the mountains, the air turned icy and the twilight fog dropped on the thickly forested slopes of Kanyal. The school suddenly acquired a remote, sequestered air, a quiet place occupied by one large family. We were lodged in a lovely cottage. Poorva Babi was right next door, and I could hear her laughing hysterically at some joke. Amar Kapoor was holed up two cottages ahead, bonding with the old boys and teachers. After hours of trudging behind Kapoor and being pushed around by the starstruck jamboree in my high-heeled boots, I was looking forward to some rest.

Inside the cottage, a sullen Chiki had already made herself at home. She had hogged half the wardrobe space, her make-up kit was littering the room, wet towels were strewn around, and the bed was all messed up. She made no attempt to move as I struggled with the equipment.

'So, madam Laila, had fun? Got your fifteen minutes with Kapoor?'

'Fun is something you should know about, darling. I am doing my work here,' I said irritably.

'Oh please, don't give *us* that, everyone is working!' Chiki's puerile fretting was puzzling. It wasn't even her shoot. She had imposed herself on our junket but was annoyed over not getting enough attention. And now her 'us' remark had created a them-and-me situation!

'Listen, I need to file a half-an-hour, so please,' I said.

'Which you got because of Nandu!'

'Which I am not denying! But it's still my half-an-hour,' I snapped at her.

Chiki backed off but I suspected there was more to follow.

'Chop chop! Now girls, please, we are guests here!' This came from Nandu, who had just walked into our room.

I changed to evening wear but the temper tantrum had

created a tense atmosphere. I stepped out and headed for the drill, a typical Rangers demonstration of physical skill by students, an old tradition that demanded rousing cheers from the stands. Amar Kapoor recalled his days as a band member.

'I did it because of the girls. You know, there were lots of good-looking ones in my batch,' he said dreamily. 'By the way, where is your fat producer?'

'Fat producer? You mean who?'

'That girl Barfee or Jalebi or Chini or whatever? The fatty.' He made crude anatomical gestures with his hand.

'You mean Chiki. She is not this show's producer,' I corrected him. 'She is my colleague and a huge fan of yours.'

'Where is she? Call her. I would like to meet her,' Amar demanded and winked at Pandey as he moved on.

I didn't bother to pass on the message. I was more interested in hearing the old yarns and tall tales. I came across a portly gentleman—Amar's classmate, as it turned out.

'Do you know, Kapoor was punished every day? The most terrible punishments were reserved for him by Bateyyr, the hostel warden.'

'Yeah? How was he punished?' I was all ears.

'Do you see that hill? Kapoor was made to go up and down every day—on his *knees*!' he added with relish.

Up ahead, I could hear Amar getting sentimental while giving a byte to a local channel.

'This school was virtually my father, my mother, my family. It was home for so many years. I am overcome with emotion.' He flicked away a tear. You almost felt for him.

Poorva Babi's entry created a flutter and boys from junior

and senior school crowded around her even as little groups of girls stood watching from a distance, exchanging whispers and staring at the Bollywood actress.

'What a ditz! A ditz with a hundred credit cards!'

There was an excited autograph and photography session interspersed with Poorva's high-pitched squeals as she met up with her old batchmates and ex-teachers. Dinner followed in the central dining hall, which erupted on Amar Kapoor's entry. The dull fare of the dining hall forgotten, the girls pressed and pushed to touch Amar, who was delighted with the attention. He scooped food off the plates of deliriously happy girls, relishing quick bites of old forgotten tastes.

By the time I returned to my room, it was quite late at night. I was checking my tapes with Nandu when Chiki came in and announced, 'I met Amar, he is a king. I love him. I told him I will sweep the floor for him if he lets me!'

Before I or Nandu could react, Chiki added, 'He has invited me to dinner. You guys can join if you want!'

Nandu and I exchanged looks, and decided to tag along with our mikes and cameraperson. You never knew what byte he would give, and maybe, finally, I would get my interview in Hindi.

When we reached his cottage, we found Amar surrounded by his gang belting out the school song *Courage is destiny*.

'Amar, can you talk about your experience, a byte in Hindi this time, please?'

'Laila, you want me to give you a byte, na? Give me a kiss first.'

'What?'

'Give me a kiss and I will give you a byte,' he repeated.

It was my cue to leave.

Peter Pan never grew up. Neither did Amar Kapoor. Early next morning, I watched boys and girls lining up to get their pappi-jhappi from Amar as he inaugurated the boxing rink and the gymnasium. The special occasion was celebrated with a vigorous display of colour, music and pageantry as boys and girls marched under the blistering midday sun.

The celebrations ended with Amar Kapoor's pearls of wisdom—hit dialogues from his blockbuster film, which the whole school repeated lustily after him. First Amar Kapoor: 'Hum keh ke nahi letey! Bas le letey hai! Kyonki nalayak hoon main!'

And then the kids, 'Nalayak hoon main! Nalayak hoon main!'

Again and again, the three words echoed through the hills of Kanyal, till the nalayak army was sufficiently impressed.

Chiki did not join us on the return trip. She said Amar would drop her off. Nandu was sure Chiki would soon move to Mumbai. Thankfully, she reached home a couple of hours after us, so we were saved from her mother's panic calls.

In a big black Hummer! Chiki texted us deliriously. *Babe, my life is changing. The shitty shoots, work and then getting arsewhipped by Bunny. It's a job for losers.*

I was almost jealous that Chiki was so focused on what she wanted. I had to deal with a boyfriend who felt ignored by me and a father who was ashamed of me. At that moment, I wished I had her life.

Crash Out

Vidya Balan's *Dirty Picture* stared soulfully from one wall and a sleazy film poster tiled *Kelewaali* peeked through the other. But my eyes were fixed on the meter that was running faster than the crappy auto. I was late for my shoot and the auto was not going fast enough.

'Bhaiyya, aapka meter tez chal raha hai. It is always fifty-seven rupees near Connaught Place's Shani temple and your auto is already showing eighty-one rupees!'

'Madam, petrol gone up! Problem hai toh doosra auto le lo,' the autowallah said, slowing down.

Bugger. I rolled my eyes and caught Salman and Katrina hugging each other on the roof of the auto.

'Arrey, bhaiyya, I am getting late. Abhi chalo.'

Rehan had been irate when I asked for an early drop in the morning. 'Why didn't you tell me before? Your shoot was later, na?' he said to me.

'Lattoo just begged and pleaded so much. She wanted to exchange the shoots. So I am going for the Mandi House film preview and she is going for my Shyamu interview.'

'But you cannot spring surprises, babe. I have a very demanding client right now and an important…'

'Listen, don't vent so much. I don't want to be in your way. Okay, I am catching an auto.' Rehan was a bad habit. It was high time I stopped being so dependent on him.

When I reached the office, Lattoo had already left for the Shyamu thingie without the list of questions that I had prepared for him, and I was trying to access her shoot details when Indu's loud wail cut short all activity.

'Oh my god! Someone is trying to jump off the roof!'

Ashen-faced Indu was furiously pointing towards the window. Nandu jumped up. Chiki dashed to the window for a better look. Within seconds, a crowd of reporters had gathered around the massive French windows on our floor, trying to look up. Some of us rushed down to the ground floor.

Perched on the ledge of the thirtieth floor was chakra healer and reiki master Ma Simmy Chabbra.

'Oh shit, it's Ma Simmy!' Indu swore.

'Ma Simmy? What happened to her? Someone should get her down!' I exclaimed.

'Shit! I had a fight with her yesterday. She misplaced my chakra sheet. I blasted her. Do you think…?' Chiki was hysterical.

'You had a tiff with her, so have half the people in this channel,' I said. 'I don't think you are responsible for this.'

Chiki looked miserable.

No one envied Simmy Chabbra's life. She opened our chakras, cleansed our auras and specialized in removing kapha, pitta, nadi and vata dosha. Most of us talked to her only when we had some dosha to remove. Or some bad energy. She was a permanent fixture in the reiki room, one of the coldest rooms in the entire building because it was right next to the main server room. Her frozen features and facial expressions never gave an insight to what was going on inside her head. She often held classes in batches, where she propounded a holistic approach to wellness. Except today. There she was, her bulky frame balanced on the slim red ledge of the thirty-first floor, legs dangling.

'Hey, what is Simmy up to?' This was Bunny. 'Fuck! Is someone up there?'

'Devika is trying to talk to her.'

'But who saw her first?'

'Simmy sent an SMS to her mother,' Shefali from the office reception interrupted. 'Her mom called the reception, sh-she told me Simmy had SMSed her that she was contemplating jumping from the building, s-so I—'

The police siren and an ambulance van's wail cut off Shefali's moment. Behind the police van, the CEO's big black Mercedes rolled in. H. Raami lunged out and glared at the little aberration on the shiny glass façade of his beloved building.

Eminent members of the world water bodies' panel, including two Nobel Prize laureates, were scheduled to participate in a discussion in the newly set up swanky studio Z. Worse, the gutkha king was expected any minute. A ruckus of this nature was the last thing H. Raami wanted. He barked out instructions to Bunny.

'Nine years. Nine frigging years in the same office and I don't know who the fuck she is. You work like a dog and this is the result. I want out of this circus as soon as I can,' Chiki voiced her angst. By now everyone had guessed where *her* angst was stemming from. No one bothered to reply.

'Laila, you going for the Raaja thingie tomorrow?' Bunny asked me.

'Bunny! I fixed the shoot, ya,' interrupted Indu. 'I have the question list ready. I need to do this.'

'Indu, perhaps you could try to look beyond your own needs and deign to consider the needs of the channel.' Bunny was at her sarcastic best. 'If Laila is the anchor of the show you have to let go some of your stars. Let's leave something for the kids. I suggest you hand over Laila your question list on Raaja.'

Bunny and Indu were almost the same age, and there were moments when Bunny loved to rub it in. It was not like Bunny was on my side or something, but I suspected she disliked Indu at a basic level.

'But Laila did not fix this. I have been slogging like shit,' Indu sulked.

'Indu, it's a half-hour sponsored slot. Why are you being so difficult,' said Bunny, irritated.

'But you sent Nandu for IIFA. He has been going for the last three years.'

'And before that you went for five straight years!' Bunny snapped. 'I also sent you to Singapore, Malaysia, Macau—no questions asked.'

'But I fixed the shoots.' Indu was unmoved.

'What the fuck do you mean *fixed*? Darling, you get the shoots because you work in EMTV. Any fucking intern can get it.'

Chiki tittered.

'What are you laughing about?' shot back Indu, now pink with embarrassment.

Before things could go out of hand we were distracted by Simmy being escorted downstairs by two bulky policewomen. The entourage was followed by a very relieved though visibly pissed H. Raami. Simmy had been coaxed off the ledge without mishap. Why she did what she did was not very clear but someone said that her mother wanted her to marry some chap whose auras and chakras did not match hers. Besides, he did not want her to continue working in a TV channel—he had a problem with the hours.

Simmy's mother, who had been widowed at a young age and had brought up Simmy, her only child, single-handedly, wanted to see her happily settled. Whether Simmy would have actually jumped off that ledge or not nobody knew—but the fact that here was an employee who, in her own twisted way, was ready to die for her job, should have amounted to something. Right? But as it turned out, Simmy was relieved of her responsibilities with immediate effect and sent off on an indefinite vacation till she got better—in short, H. Raami fired her.

Indu was still mad at Chiki, but it was too late and Bunny didn't give a damn. So she was mad at me too. She gave me a nasty look and stormed off without handing over her question list. I did not mind one bit. Besides, Nandu would help me with the questions. I stayed late for some research on Raaja, and missed the dinner date with Rehan's family. Rehan was miffed but I was sure I could make it up to him later. I was too excited.

I was meeting superstar Raaja Babu.

Headline

*We have more possibilities available in each moment than
we realize.*

— THICH NHAT HANH, ZEN MONK

He glided in and waved to the crowd on cue. His lithe
body had an agility that belied his age. His every move
was followed by the mesmerized crowd. He stood with his
legs apart, spread his arms, threw back his head, thumped
his hips back and forth—first two slow thrusts and then,
with a gigantic heave, his trademark pelvic thrust. The
crowd roared in orgasmic relief.

With a hundred eyes fixed on his now famous crotch, not
counting the millions watching on television, he performed
the act—a massive pelvic thrust again and again as the crowds
erupted in approval.

R-A-A-J-A!

R-A-A-J-A!

The big boss of splendour and pomp, Bollywood's superstar Raaja Babu ruled the collective conscience of manoranjan and entertainment news like no other star. Every quirk of his, from his swagger to his stutter, his hairstyle, dialogue delivery, even his way of romancing, was a sellout. Raaja Babu was a master of the game when it came to wooing the media.

'See, I am getting goose bumps,' said Gogol, a die-hard Raaja fan. He even had an autographed 'I am from Raaja's Planet' T-shirt which, rumour had it, he kept under his pillow.

'I don't know what you see in Raaja uncle!' Saryu said, unimpressed.

'OMG! Don't say that in front of Gogol—you have been warned—but you're right. Maybe he is looking a little gaunt and old,' I said.

Today, at the age of fifty-eight, Raaja Babu was facing his biggest nemesis—rapidly failing health. Pure adrenalin goes only so far. A chain smoker, heavily into stimulants and addicted to painkillers after a neck injury, the star was slowly becoming a shadow of his former self. Long absences from the big screen had given rise to speculation on the beginning of the fall of the superstar.

'A whole bunch of hungry actors half his age was snapping at his heels. That can't be a very good feeling!' said Saryu.

'Puhleeze! He has shrines built in his name, he is the *boss*,' Gogol said.

It was the launch of a well-known international car brand, and despite being unwell and suffering from a crippling neck pain, Raaja had made time for his generous sponsors.

'He is getting eight crore rupees,' informed Shivani from P Channel.

'No, yaar! Five crore was what he took to dance for fifteen minutes at that Delhi businessman's daughter's sangeet. He must be taking much more here,' declared Gogol with authority.

'Look, he is here.'

As Raaja Babu descended from the stage, I realized he was definitely thinner than the last time I had interviewed him. The bones on his face were jutting out against almost paper-thin skin, his eyes were ablaze with an icy fire. Curiously, he reminded me of a Zen monk I had met in Ladakh. Tranquil and peaceful, gleefully enjoying the raging storm we were caught in. Those eyes, I reminded myself, had driven millions of men and women crazy. I quickly went over the questions I had to ask the Bollywood star.

Bunny's brief was clear: 'Get him to talk for sixteen minutes and you have your half-hour.'

With the chain of Hulk Hogans circling him protectively, getting a byte, let alone an interview, seemed impossible. Photographers and cameramen pushed in mad frenzy. One overzealous print cameraman lost his footing and almost fell on Raaja Babu. In a second, the hapless guy was pinned down by the monstrous bouncers. But it was the star who helped the dishevelled cameraman get up. A million flashes, and the moment was eternalized.

'Tu baad mein aana. Meri jitni photo utaarni hai tu utar lena! Tu jaise pose bolega main doonga! Come later, I will pose the way you want me to, theek hai? Now, should I go?' The great Raaja Babu talking to a cameraman!

'Shhhhhh, he is saying something... Please, sir, can you repeat?'

He repeated, 'Tu baad mein aana. Meri jitni photo utaarni hai tu utar lena! I will pose especially for you! Now, should I go?'

'Record kiya. Abbey, audio liya?'

'Liyaa... liyaa. Done.'

'Sir, once more. Sir, ek baar aur!'

And he delivered once again. The superstar's generosity re-clicked, re-captured, re-recorded from every angle. The media cheered and Raaja Babu moved on.

'He stoops to conquer. So shall run my show donut,' I said.

As he passed me I blurted out, 'Raaja, five minutes please.'

A coffee-addict-cum-chain-smoker's teeth smiled back through the fleshy cage of bouncers. Enough to put anyone off. But the eyes were magnetic.

'Ya, sweetheart, sure! Just let me get this over with, but why don't you talk to Alka over there,' a polished voice smelling of cognac and coffee and expensive cigarettes rang out.

Dour-faced Alka, till now an irritating shadow on the camera lens, suddenly zoomed in. She blushed behind her huge horn-rimmed glasses.

'Hey, Alkaah! Tu kitni patli ho gayee! Slim and sexxxxy. I will have to speak to your husband.' Raaja shook his finger in mock admonishment and Alka, stuffed into her squeaky new office suit, squealed in delight. This was what was special about

Raaja Babu—he remembered little things like your name and what you did and complimented you, adding a personal touch to whatever he said. Hearing the exchange, the goggle-eyed media looked at Alka with interest.

Alka shooed us media walas out of the room into the dimly let corridor where we had no choice but to wait out our turn with the star. Only choice channels would make it inside the star's sanctorum, it was announced.

'Stand in line, please,' Alka commanded. Not wanting to annoy the PR lady-turned-goddess of Raaja Babu's earthly affairs, we blurted out our names for the roll call. Stumbling TRPs for EMTV meant being placed rather low in the interview order, but I was in no hurry. I did have the big star in my bag… this would keep Bunny sated for a couple of days. I headed for the ante-room.

First things first: make-up. I perched on a corner chair to get my face fixed. Balancing my big mirror between my legs—first came the Mac Studio Fix NC40 for my face. It did wonders for my sallow complexion, a make-up expert had assured me. Next came the Body Shop Shimmer Cubes Lumiere. I settled for dusted gold for my eyes to set off the gold pattern on my outfit. I sprayed my musky Rika Ajmal perfume. The final touch: Strawberry Blonde A-98 luscious lip gloss, my one indulgence from my DA money at the last Dubai film festival. Gone were the days when I would have shied away from combing my hair in public—these days, I didn't give a damn. I tried a smile into my mirror… the professional let's-get-on-with-the-job smile, or would I go with the slightly nervous I-am-so-in-awe-of-your-splendour smile? It did bring out the chivalry in most men.

When my turn came and I entered planet Raaja, a silence that whispered tremendous success and immense money surrounded him. Raaja Babu was sitting on a plush black sofa wearing a smile and his favourite black Armani silk shirt and dark grey trousers, a dark red tie breaking the monochromatic palette. He looked at me and smiled.

There was no distraction once you entered the superstar's sanctorum. His focus on you was complete. Pinned under his frank gaze, I forgot my opening line.

'Hello, Raaja,' I said finally.

What was it? What was the opening line? *With me is the man who… no, no, shit.*

'Hello, Laila dear. Sit down, please.' Raaja Babu gave me his trademark smile.

Lord! That sexy cleft.

The PR girl whispered, 'Just fifteen minutes, remember.' Shivam slipped the mike lapel on Raaja Babu and did the final audio check.

What, what do I say in my opening line? *The man with the profile… god!*

'Has it become a fad to hate you?' I blurted out.

'My fans love me, Laila. Don't you.' It was not a question.

'Enough has been said about your ongoing war of words with your co-star Munjal. He has accused you of chopping off his role in your new film because you are also the producer. How do you respond to that accusation?'

Raaja was sweating, his eyes started watering alarmingly and his hands turned clammy. But it had nothing to do with me or my question. Two men suddenly interrupted and took over. My cameraman and I were asked to leave for a few minutes as Raaja had to be given his medication. When I finally returned, Raaja looked more alert. A slight trace of white near his upper lip revealed hurriedly taken medication. I had been warned by the PR person not to risk upsetting Raaja by asking him questions about his health.

'As you said, enough has been said. Baseless things. There is no war like the media makes it out to be. He is doing his job, I am doing mine. Munjal is a good friend.'

The eyes were still watery but lord, that cleft on his chin was dishy.

'You know, the media should focus on the positive aspect, the good work that I do.' His eyes bore into mine. 'Instead of Raaja and Munjal fighting, or Munjal not inviting me to his party, or Raaja did not look at Munjal, usne mooh tedha kiya, kyon kiya…? Come on, what's all this? Thats not the way it works,' Raaja admonished me. I felt as guilty as a twelve-year-old caught with a dirty magazine.

The sourpuss PR Alka was, meanwhile, waving a sheet of paper furiously, indicating that I stick to questions about the brand. I ignored her.

'Munjal said his pet rabbit is the biggest Raaja. How do you react?' I said.

The superstar's eyes turned a shade darker. But the cleft remained intact.

'That's his love. His rabbit can be Raaja, my turtle can be Munjal, so what? We are all animals, right? Ha ha!' As if on cue, Raaja's entourage burst out laughing and the star raised his hand to silence them.

'I want to say for once and for all that I love him. He is my brother, and brothers fight, don't they? I am sure you fight with your brother.'

'All the time!'

'You know, the other day I met Leonardo DiCaprio…'

Very quietly, I sneaked in the question I was dying to ask. 'What about the Soorma brothers?'

'What about them? And why are you asking *me*? Half the people in Bollywood know them!'

The Soormas were political biggies. They owned malls, hotels and cinema halls across the country. When the Soormas threw parties, the who's who of Bollywood attended. Recently, Raaja Babu had signed on as brand ambassador of their swanky real estate venture. The problem was that the Soormas were now in major trouble after their names had come up in the biggest land scam in Mumbai. The CBI had accused them of hoarding black money to the tune of 1,500 crore rupees in benaami accounts.

'They are your good friends.'

'Of course.' He was curt.

'But their name has come up in this land scam—'

'Okay, okay, you have to wrap up *now*!' Raaja's PR machinery swung into action.

'I have so many friends. I don't think you know what you are talking about, girl, get your facts right. Let's talk about what I like! I love the sound of young beautiful girls like you screaming out my name.'

'Chalo, chalo, time is up.' Alka was jumping up and down in anxiety.

'You know, you need to get away from sensationalism in reporting!' Raaja's words stopped me in my tracks. 'Your channel EMTV used to have a very different standard of reporting, not this snoopy tabloid journalism.'

And almost instantly, I became all that was wrong with the television industry today.

⚘

Hi, Laila, I suggest you leave out the Soorma angle. This SMS from Alka left me mystified. I had already reached office and was wondering why Alka had waited for me to leave the location before texting.

But why?

Sweetie, because they are unverified reports! You will not get away with this kind of irresponsible reporting! Alka wrote condescendingly.

I think you should let me decide what I want to report and what I don't, I wrote back tersely.

And so I went ahead with the Raaja-Soorma connection as my lead story. And I was very happy with my irreverent script and the cheeky edit.

My happiness did not last long.

'What was that choot story? When will you get it? Don't take panga with superstars. You know the show Raaja Babu had promised to do with us is in jeopardy?' Bunny screamed.

'What? But why?' I asked.

'Laila, you know why! Considering it's your little piece that led to this mess. Raaja has sent an SMS to H. Raami—what was the need to do an investigative thingie between Raaja and

Soorma? Last I checked, you were an entertainment hack. Or have you changed your beat?'

'But Bunny, didn't H. Raami say he wanted our scripts to be irreverent?' I tried to cut in.

'Shut up. Gutkha king called. He wants to know who the fuck filed that story. Worse, he wants to know who the fuck cleared that story!'

'But—'

'Shut up. You fool, do you know Raaja was to launch gutkha king's new reality show?'

'But—'

Not only do I have to save your sorry arse again, I have to beg Raaja to continue being the brand ambassador for our *Citizens Speak Up Now* show.'

'But you can see the script, there is nothing in it that isn't true,' I insisted.

'Forget it. Your story is dead. It is off air. I have already told the PCR to add a promo to fill the show duration. Now scoot!'

Not only was my story taken off air but Nandu was appointed by Bunny to oversee all my stories editorially.

I was officially in the doghouse.

It had been two years since I joined as an entertainment reporter in EMTV. Every day, the first people I called were PR agents. Pubs had become my daily haunts; sexy cinema lounges, swanky watering holes, the plushest restro-bars, the most exclusive night clubs, the A-list discotheques—actually even the seedy ones—were launched only after they had told me about it! I got hundreds of calls every day. Fashion designers pushing their collections, event managers peddling their 'star-studded' events, PR agents selling their stars, art galleries promising a Bollywood invitee, it was never ending. I even got invites from aunties calling me to their farmhouse for their kid's birthday party. I had no inhibitions. I had covered everything from star idiosyncrasies and diamond-dripping mehendi ceremonies to pretentious baby showers with sparkling kids on display. I had covered dog shows, Halloween parties, kitty and card parties, ice cream launches, pizza- and pastry-making competitions, film premieres and star interviews. Every day I waited for that big sexy story. It came but rarely; on most days, my stories were confined to '... and, finally'.

But I had my *Filmy Masti* show and it got five repeats a day. I am sure that amounts to something.

Flash It

I had always thought Chiki would be the first person to bail out from EMTV. But as it happened, it was Latika. Shyamu Sharma had offered Latika a break in his new untitled film. Latika had interviewed the director several times, but clearly it was she who had left more than a lasting impression on him. We should have suspected something was going on when Shyamu started insisting that Bunny send only Latika to take his interviews.

'My role will be parallel to that of the lead heroine's!' Lattoo gushed, her almond eyes sparkling with excitement.

'But what do you know about acting?' Chiki asked.

'Arrey, same as every heroine. Anyway, Shyamu says he will get me enrolled in some acting workshop.'

'Shyamu says! Did you get that? Look… ab tu Shyamu ke liye naachegi?' Nandu, who was just back from IIFA, teased Latika mercilessly. 'Lattoo badnaam hui, daarrling Shyamu ke liye!'

'But Lattoo, are you sure you can trust this offer? I mean, what if you chuck this shit for Mr Shyamu's promised pot of gold but land up in a bigger load of shit?' Indu certainly had a way with words.

But Latika was firm about her plans to leave EMTV to follow her Bollywood ambitions.

'But what about your anchoring?' I asked. 'Bunny was saying she was thinking of giving you a weekend show now?'

'Screw Bunny. Babe, I am going to Bollywood.' Lattoo was ecstatic.

'Aur tera French boyfriend?' Chiki asked Lattoo.

'The dude is British,' Nandu corrected Chiki.

'Whatever!'

'So, *Maya*, when are you off, madam?' Indu asked.

'Maya?' We looked at her.

'She didn't tell you? That's her new screen name! Lattoo is Maya now,' Indu revealed with relish.

'You are kidding me, dude! Lattoo, who gave you that name? Don't tell me it's your Shyamu babu,' Nandu said.

Latika smiled sheepishly.

'Lattoo, Shyamu Sharma's last four films flopped! Why are you so desperate to join him?' Indu asked.

'Shut up, Indu, stop freaking her out! For once, can't you be happy for someone?' Chiki's eyes blazed. 'The kid is trying to do something new.'

'You know, Chiki, you should stop playing Lattoo's mommy, now that she is going out into the big bad world.'

'And you have a hope in hell of getting into Bollywood. Actually, maybe Shyamu can fit you in one of his bhoot films. I can see it now: best debut chudail award for Indu.'

'Oh! What about your ticket to Bollywood? Didn't Mr Amar Kapoor... er... send for you? Or is it like raat gayee baat gayee?' Indu smirked.

'Indu, be bloody careful what you say!' Chiki's five-feet-eleven-inch frame towered over Indu. Red-faced and furious, Chiki looked ready to hit her.

'Break it up now,' hollered Bunny. 'What the fuck is happening on this desk? And Lattoo or Maya or whatever, you may be a celebrity, but can you please let us jantaa get this side circus over with? Laila, is the run order ready? Where are you doing your links for tonight's show? Nandu, collect your DA from accounts. You are going to New Zealand, read your mail sometimes, ya! Indu, Chiki, in my cabin, now.'

After Bunny's outburst, Latika left abruptly. I did not know then but this was my last face-to-face meeting with Latika. She would be Maya the next time I met her. Bunny's abruptness with Lattoo was puzzling. Hadn't she wanted Latika out in the first place?

There was no farewell party for Lattoo. But her departure did not shock me as much as Rehan's did.

Unity Tanking, Server Malfunctioning

It started with me being mad at Rehan. Hopping mad. I had caught him going through the texts on my mobile. I mean, there was nothing to hide, but Rehan was being pig-headed about a few things. Like, he wanted to know why Nandu called me a gazillion times every day.

'But what does it mean, *black suits you, hottie?*' Rehan read out an SMS loudly.

'It means precisely that—that black suits me! I was looking good in the show today! Why the fuck is it such a bother?'

I found it very irritating that at 3.25 a.m., I was having a discussion about Nandu's mental construct with Rehan.

'How would you react if a girl sent me an SMS like that?'

'But he is not like that; he is Nandu, why are you being so obtuse?'

'He is not like that? What is this?'

'Arrey, Rehan, it's just for laughs.'

'I would love to see what sort of SMSes you are sending

him for laughs. You can be really dumb, men are the same beyond a point.'

'Hey, that's rich, Rehan. You are FBing the world all the time and I don't even use my FB account. That's how much I socialize! When was the last time you saw me party with my deskies? I don't smoke. I hardly drink. I don't even go to office parties. I am like this worker ant, dude. I go to work, I come back. I have no time for sex. I sleep early so that I can go to work early. I guess that makes me really dumb!'

'Thanks for the crash course on your virtues. I would love you even if you sinned a little. But this Nandu texting at 3 a.m., I can't stand.'

'Listen, what do you think my job is? Do you think I am getting paid to indulge in free fuckathons? Nandu is interested in only one person, and that's himself. Baal ki khaal mat nikaalo, yaar. You know me, right? This discussion is plain idiotic.'

'Yeah, lots of things happening right now are plain idiotic.'

'For instance?'

Rehan was quiet.

I could feel my stomach tightening. Rehan did not rake up idiotic issues at 3 a.m. without good reason—he had taken some decision and he was troubled about breaking it to me.

'Really, what's bothering you, Rehan? Out with it,' I said lightly.

'You know that telecom project in East Africa—the one I had pitched for?'

'Yeah?'

'It's come through. I am going to Nairobi.'

'You are?' (Oh, no.)

'It's a two-year deputation.'

'Hmm? Okay.' (Bloody shit.)

The room had suddenly become suffocating. I wanted to sit down.

'You can come if you want to,' he said.

'You know that's not possible.' (He did not say, 'I want you to come' but 'You can come if you want to'—what did that mean?)

'Laila, take a sabbatical. You have worked hard.'

'Not hard enough! I can't go now. There's too much stuff happening.' (Living without Rehan? But why wasn't he insisting I go with him?)

'How will you live alone? You have no idea how to run a house,' Rehan said.

'Living alone is not the issue. (What the fuck am I doing? Stop him, Laila. Stop him now. Beg.) I can shift to PG accommodation. Suniti and Trisha from office are desperately looking for a pad.'

I felt drained. Rehan's face was impassive. He must have been hoping against hope. But what about my hopes? Bunny was becoming sort of okay with me now, and I had made it to special correspondent. If I left now, where would I be? Cases of women bailing out for a chance at an alternate life were unheard of in EMTV. Probably because most hacks were too busy to have a life. But I digress.

Bunny had warned me that there were fifty girls ready to take my place. Besides, Rehan hadn't tried very hard to convince me to go with him. If he didn't care, why should I?

Chunk It

'Chaddhi pehni hai usne?' The cameraman's casual remark left me acutely embarrassed. Jammed firmly between camerapersons built like bulls, I had no place to go. It was a packed press conference for a big budget Bollywood film starring Vicky Kumar, whose last film *Bloody Fools* had been a big hit.

As the cameramen discussed the starlet in question and her underwear, I stared ahead stone-facedly, desperately hoping for the press conference to begin and their *Basic Instinct* moment to pass. The underwear had recently become a fashion casualty with several Bollywood starlets going without it. What could have prompted this trend? Perhaps they felt more comfy around the crotch (as Yana Gupta had said) or imagined their little black numbers sitting more snugly on their butt (as per Shamita Shetty). Whatever the reason, the niggling piece of cloth had been done away with.

The object of today's crude exchange was an exotic import from Brazil who was making her Bollywood debut. The starlet, sitting on the dais some twenty feet away, was a suspect since she had a bit of a reputation for risque fashion statements and a penchant to dump the drawers.

'Why is she sitting in such a weird pose? Is she trying to hide something?' the X News guy asked.

'Pehni hai. Red hai. Matches her dress,' came the official verdict.

'Saala itni garmi hai room ke andar; maar dega garmi mein.'

'Shuru karo, yaar.'

'Please shift up.'

'Sorry. We came first,' said the P News cameraman, who had come with two camera assistants and one light man.

'Abbey, why have you got an army with you? Yahaan bhi 33 per cent reservation soch ke aaya hai kya?' someone shouted.

The hall broke into a nervous titter. A PR girl with a just-out-of-school expression cleared her throat.

'Madam, popcorn hi de do. What about some thanda Coke-shoke?'

The hassled PR girl could not have gone more wrong in her choice of attire for her coming-out day: a ghastly grey pencil-slim skirt that was riding up her thigh, revealing nude stockings and a white slip—a recipe for disaster and major embarrassment, and it only made her more self-conscious.

'Hey, look!' nudged photog Manoj. 'Uski phat rahi hai!'

The PR girl was running between reporters in the crowded room. I cringed at her plight. She faced the prospect of climbing up and down the podium with the collective Indian media watching, some even recording.

'Arrey, why are you recording her?' someone asked.

'Cutaways, baba!' Manoj winked.

But the side circus did not distract me for long. I spotted Saryu cosying up to the star's PR, Monica. It was not for nothing that Saryu had earned her reputation as the city's principle PR schmoozer. She would schmooze, cheat, grab, beg, do whatever it took to get interviews with stars. Monica had been an ex-entertainment tabloid hack for seven years and switched sides from reportage to PR during recession. Today she had top-notch actors including Vicky Kumar as her clients. Saryu had obviously pataaoed Monica, as the two were busy air-kissing each other.

'Man, is he short,' my cameraperson echoed my thoughts as Vicky Kumar glided into the packed room, his smooth walk matching his demeanour.

'I miss that I-am-in-front-of-a-superstar feeling,' Princey whined.

'Only Raaja does it for Princey!'

'Vicky is done to death.'

'Overdose ho gaya. Kitna chalayenge. *Bloody Fools* hit hai yaar, khatam karo!'

'I think he has put on weight again.'

'Yeah, I agree! I am going with it, anyway. Vicky ho gaya mota!'

Vicky's shrewd eyes darted about as he took in the crowded room. He was accompanied by the loud-mouthed producer Siddhu Khurana, who was wearing a cheesy smile. Siddhu had something of a corner seat on super-hit comedies. Vicky answered each question with an indulgent smile plastered on his face.

He moved his hands a lot. He touched his lips. He made eye contact with reporters. He was the most compelling actor I had ever met. I thought of all the hundreds of crores this diminutive Kumar had minted in his last film—the gargantuan super-duper hit *Bloody Fools*. The film's satellite rights itself had gone for a whopping 80 crore rupees, apart from the 150 crore rupees the film had already made.

'Vicky, Vicky, this side. How do you manage to look so young?'

'Oh, no, he will take ages on this one,' I groaned.

'… and then I went into the mind of a teenager. I thought young. It's incredible. My body language changed my—'

'Vicky, who are the bloody fools in Bollywood?'

'Hey, how would I know? I am only a bloody fool!' Vicky said.

'How does someone so average-looking make so much money,' I muttered.

Vicky's honey-brown eyes looked around. He seemed taken aback by the huge media presence.

The problem was this: The room easily had thirty-five TV, radio, cable channel and print media with their photogs—which meant that each actor would be doing a minimum of thirty-five interviews in Hindi and in English. Vicky Kumar had put his foot down and refused to do one-on-ones except with one Hindi and two English channels, and one from print.

The reporters were understandably pissed.

'Achha tamasha hai—why were we called then?'

'Why are you doing two English channels, why not two Hindi ones? He is a Hindi film hero, isn't he?' The frustrated crowd of hacks started pushing towards the stars.

'Guys, please move back! We have to think of the audience too,' Monica yelled.

'Hello madam, Vicky's real audience is the Hindi masses.'

'We will not go like this, khaali haath!'

Seated on a raised podium, Vicky Kumar tried to look cool and in control. Some hack from a local cable TV channel sized me up nervously. I knew she wanted to stick her mike next to mine so that her interview was assured. EMTV still had a formidable reputation in the market.

'What's your job then? Why are you a special correspondent? I might as well send an intern; use your PR skills if you still possess any,' Bunny had thundered at me. 'I want the actors' arses on the 8 p.m. bulletin, or it's your arse.'

Bunny had not factored in three things:

One: TRPs determine where you are slotted by the PR in the interview list. Low TRPs for our channel in the last two quarters had changed the game for us. We were no longer *the* channel every star wanted to do first. As reporters, we were well aware of the changing equations but convincing the desk, which seemed to inhabit a different time zone, was another matter altogether.

Two: The demand for entertainment by news channels had mutated hacks into vicious news hounds. Greedy hacks fresh out of school waiting to bite and take the mike out of you abounded… so it was youth versus reliability, grit versus glamour, and the scales often tilted in favour of youth and glamour. Channels had resorted to hiring fresh-out-of-school trainees. At three underpaid eager-to-please hungry freshers for the price of one experienced reporter, these kids were saving channels lots of money. Experienced reporters like Saryu, Gogol and I found ourselves competing with hyperactive cub reporters almost half our age. The rite of passage had served to make their reportage even more visceral and guttural. Getting an exclusive in this scenario was not going to be a cakewalk.

Three: This was a personal failing. The inability to schmooze. I had awakened a little late to the new gods, the PR agents. Nothing was possible without them, and nothing impossible with them. You could be a ball-breaking reporter but in a world ruled by two words—public relations—nothing of consequence could be arranged without their nod.

I had been dumbed down to the number four spot, which meant, as per schedule, that the one-on-one seemed dicey. I caught Saryu winking at her cameraman. Saryu's channel was at par with EMTV, but she had obviously managed to get some sort of deal. I stuffed my mini-DVC in my pocket and with mike in hand, I pushed towards Monica.

'Hi, Monica,' I began.

'Sweetie, forget it today—look at all these reporters. If I give you Vicky, I will have to give him to each one of them, ya,' Monica said and shuddered. I did not want to dwell on my last interaction with Monica, about five years ago—an ugly war of words on the merits of a Hindi film that she was promoting and I was reviewing. Monica had wanted me to change the dismal ratings I had given to the film, and promised an exclusive with another Bollywood superstar—naturally, I had blasted her for thinking she could dictate terms to an EMTV reporter. In my defence, those were my early days of reporting when my head was still full of romantic notions about my trade. Monica never gave me the first call for any of her stars' interviews after that.

'No chance today, unless you wished Monica on her dog's birthday,' said Gogol, looking pleased as punch—he was slotted first with Vicky Kumar.

Truth: Every PR guy is actually a gossip-churning publicist. What they really want is to pass off as king makers and media futurists. Catering to the 'jo dikhta hai, woh bikta hai' dictum, these spin doctors turn, twist, tweak, plant, plug and conceal stories to suit their star clients. Their ubiquitous talent for crisis management is useful for diverting media attention from unpleasant events in an actor's life.

Crisis entered just then in the form of Arindam Pillai. Vicky's smile froze. Even Siddhu Khurana was left gaping at the entrance.

Arindam Pillai was a little known producer from down south. He had made a film called *The Bloody Rascals*. Arindam had accused Vicky and Siddhu Khurana of plagiarizing his film *The Bloody Rascals* and making *Bloody Fools*. Arindam swore he had not given the filmmakers the rights to his film, and now that the film was a hit, he thought he had a right to cash in on the profits. He was also miffed that he had not been invited to the premiere of the film he said he had conceived. Now he wanted 2.5 crore rupees as compensation. But neither Vicky nor his producers were ready to pay Arindam a single paisa.

As the moments passed, Vicky looked more strained and Siddhu more sulky. Arindam had entered the presser with a determined expression and sat down purposefully on a vacant chair, waiting for his turn to ask questions. He was staring at Vicky and Siddhu as if daring them to throw him out in the presence of the media.

Vicky was struggling to keep the smile on his face. Siddhu was frowning openly. Someone had thoughtfully handed Arindam the mike. He cleared his throat to speak.

'Hello, distinguished members of the media. I am Arindam Pillai. Some of you, my dear friends, know me. I am not a big star or a big producer but I am proud of the little work I have done. Among them was a film very close to my heart. *The Bloody Rascals*,' Arindam said. '*The Bloody Rascals* is *my* baby,' he added, standing up. 'I want to ask why was my baby, *The Bloody Rascals*, hijacked and made into *Bloody Fools* without my permission? Without a single paisa coming my way? Do you, sirs, think I am a bloody fool to allow this?' This last was directed at Vicky and Siddhu.

I lost everything else in the din that followed.

Siddhu, who had been struggling to stay in his chair, suddenly blew a fuse and almost bounced off the podium.

'Shut up, *shut up!*' Siddhu exclaimed.

'Oh my god… what just happened?'

'Did he say rascal?'

'Did he say bloody fool?'

'Did he say shut up?'

'Shut up, *shut up!*' Siddhu screamed maniacally.

A very embarrassed Vicky Kumar tried his best to get the raging Siddhu to calm down.

'I hope you're rolling,' I nudged my cameraperson.

Arindam Pillai had asked the one question that was on everyone's agenda. Vicky's attempts to pacify Siddhu seemed to irritate the producer even more. He shrugged off Vicky's hand and yelled at Arindam, 'You are a cheat, a bastard. I want this bugger out, now…'

Whatever else the hapless Arindam was expecting, it certainly was not this.

The press was divided. People were shouting. The celebration was turning into a squabble with some sections booing the others, even as Arindam was forcibly evicted by Vicky's bouncers. The media protested loudly as they had not had the chance to take Arindam's bytes.

'How dare he say shut up?'

'He has to apologize.'

'He can't behave like this.'

'Oh god, Siddhu has lost it.'

'This is so uncivilized…'

'We should boycott this.'

'No, we will file this… let's take his pants off, man!'

'Oooooh, this is good… how should I super this?'

Meanwhile, another commotion broke out. Saryu, who had tried to take Arindam Pillai's byte on his way out, had just punched Vicky's bouncer. And he had slapped her back. Within seconds, there was a huge uproar with the media pushing aggressively towards the bouncer and hollering at the

PR. The overzealous security man, while trying to keep the press at bay, had, in the process, knocked down poor Saryu with his long limbs.

There were two versions of the fight at this point—one was that the bouncer started laughing after pushing her and Saryu had simply retaliated, after which the bouncer attacked her.

The other version, the one presented by the PR, maintained that Saryu had kicked the bouncer and given some ma-behen ki gaali, and the bouncer, a simple Jat from Haryana, was telling her to be quiet when he lost his balance and his hands touched her face accidentally.

'Yeah, right!'

'How dare he hit a female reporter!'

'Saala! We will boycott the presser.'

'Boss, yeh nahi chalega.'

'I will complain to the producer… Where is that Monica?'

'I will file an FIR!' screeched Saryu.

'Monica, what is this?' Vicky shouted.

'Vicky can go home—no one is doing the interviews,' the media threatened.

'I am not taking this. Be ready for my police complaint against the organizers and that bastard bouncer. You think you can have your goondas pounce on female reporters like that?' Saryu fumed.

For Monica, things were rapidly going from bad to out of control. The event was turning out to be a PR disaster of catastrophic proportions. A reporter was sobbing. A producer had to be thrown out. Another producer was seething. The press was up in arms. The stars were unhappy.

Vicky was particularly upset. This was the first leg of the ambitious promotions he had planned for his film, but after such a catastrophe, the entire promotion tour was marred. After all, the same channels had been invited to cover the rest of his tour, and Vicky was afraid he would end up explaining today's tamasha at every event till his film released.

'Monica, if your bouncer apologizes to the media, and Vicky and the whole cast agree to do one-on-ones with every channel, perhaps you can salvage something. I mean, we all have to take something back, right?' I proposed to Monica.

A shaken Monica would have agreed to anything at this point. Saryu calmed down after the bouncer's apology, and was already going through her question list. We left long before Vicky could hope to leave.

Back in office, Bunny was uncharacteristically disinterested in my ordeal. 'So what? The market has tanked—at least try to be aware of what's happening beyond your story! Your Ram katha has been dropped,' she informed me casually. Just like that. 'I don't think the news wants a package also... just make a small one-minuter—or chuck it, leave it for a rainy day. What I want to know from you is, do you know Antim?' Bunny's question threw me.

'Antim? That new anchor? Doesn't he do Rene's show?' I asked. I recalled Antim's pasty face in the make-up room, bitching about Rene. Not the sort I would want to run into if the lights went out. Come to think of it, not even when the lights were on.

'Yes. The same gent.'

'Yes, I do—I mean, Latika introduced me to him. Why?'

'Antim was caught inside the women's loo in that nightclub in CP—Rene was also there…'

'What was he doing?' I said.

'Editing. Discussing next year's fucking run order. Stupid! He had his pants down…They were at it!' Bunny said.

'Wha—oh!'

'The camera next to the toilet caught them going inside and not coming out for a looooong time—the admin girl is saying they were at it,' Bunny said evilly. 'Get me some details na, from your friends upstairs—use your PR!'

Breaking In

Before I go any further, I want to tell you what happened to Latika.

For a long time Latika had been treated as the resident ditz of the EMTV Bolly desk. In the last few months, Bunny had become indifferent to her. This was a far cry from the fuss made over her when she joined a year ago, straight from some exotic UK university. Boys from the floors above looked for excuses to come to the tenth floor to catch a glimpse of the new stunner. Bunny did something she never did: she treated everyone to free lunch. But then Latika was not meant to be ordinary; she had the air of a star biding her time.

My first reaction when I saw her was that of utter dismay. She was armed with the smile of an angel and the body of a diva. She was too short to be a model, but what she lacked in centimetres she made up for with inches in all the right places. In short, she was stunning. It was obvious why H. Raami had hired her, but why the hard-nosed Bunny agreed to take her on our desk puzzled me. I could not visualize Latika running around with tapes, waiting for stars, or even writing scripts. I guess the channel needed a star.

Thankfully there was more to life in EMTV than looks. And that's where Latika stopped and the rest of us began.

The first thing we did to get over Latika's otherworldly beauty was to rename her Lattoo. It made her more human. Lattoo's redeeming quality was that she was always unfazed. She was a natural. The ogling, the attention, the cat calls, the mesmerized boys, the miffed girls... nothing bothered her. Bunny took it upon herself to mentor Latika, she gave her prime shoots, prime slots and prepared her for anchoring.

But it was clear from day one that she was not meant to be a news reporter. Bunny gave her many second chances. But weakly written scripts, incomplete shoots, bad interviews, a cavalier attitude and the worst bloopers soon ate into Bunny's patience and had her screaming bloody murder. It dawned on Bunny that her London import had zero Hindi-speaking skills, less than zero English-writing skills, and a very questionable intent to learn anything about news. As punishment, Bunny consigned Latika to slave duty—calling up stars, fixing interviews, writing tickers and publishing stories. It was embarrassing for Bunny to admit she had made a mistake.

What no one knew was that Latika never made mistakes. The way I see it now is that Lattoo was basically getting her Bollywood connections in place. Within weeks she had made a formidable diary of Bolly contacts.

At the first opportunity, she copped out without a backward glance. Today, she was in seventh heaven.

This is what she had dreamt of. The screen test at Shyamu's was a lark. She did not have to do anything extraordinary. For some strange reason, Shyamu continued to be enamoured by her and that was just as well, till her first film released. She had bigger plans for herself. She wanted to be famous, and fast. To see her name on billboards, have channels fighting over her bytes, cameras waiting for her for hours… Latika was giddy with happiness. Bunny apologizing to her would have been the icing on the cake.

Now, if only Shyamu gave her that big item number. Something hot and sexy to herald her entry into mayanagari. The problem was item queen Shabby blocking her way into B-town with her big fat arse.

Tracks Offline

It was a messed-up week. Too much confusion. Long days. Empty nights. Even since Rehan left for Nairobi.

And then there were papa's calls.

'But why would you not go with Rehan?'

'I—'

'There is TV in Nairobi too and better channels. You could get a job there.'

'I have a career here, papa.'

'You are impossible. What sort of show is *Filmy Masti*? What do you hope to achieve by running after idiotic stars? They are all nautankiwalas! Is that what you want in life?'

'I—'

'What bewaqufi are you doing? Rehan was the one decent thing in your life.'

I slammed the phone down finally. I was at a loss for words. Decent words, that is.

To make matters worse, there was a recession. All over India, employees from private companies were being fired left, right and centre. I heard horrifying stories from other TV channels. Some reporter whose mother was in hospital had been fired, and she had no money to pay the bills. A library guy who was to get married next month had been fired. An award-winning cameraman who was on his way back from a strenuous shoot was told to submit the tapes and collect his termination letter. Lots of newcomers and some veterans who had been in the industry for years were suddenly jobless.

Surprisingly, EMTV remained 'recession-proof' for the longest time. Our merry band of reporters spent a lot of time happily taking bytes from Bollywood stars on recession.

Recession? What's the worst that could happen to us?

'... kya kehna hai recession ke baare mein?'

'... what should be recession-proof?'

'... how do you feel now that you can't buy that swanky new Hummer?'

And the joke was on us. It knocked the air out of everyone. It started with H. Raami's ominous emails...

... lazybones, clean up your acts.

... foot draggers will not be tolerated.

... dawdlers, beware, we have the dope on you.

(Of course, not in these words exactly!)

Just as unexpectedly, furious shit hit the fan. The gutkha king was having second thoughts about the channel and wanted to slash overheads. He wanted to invest in kitchen masalas. Harindranath Raami's next communication caused a lot of heart burn. Everyone's salary was to be slashed by 40 per cent. The nightmare just kept getting worse. After the slashed salaries came the firings.

Everyone was really scared. But thankfully the already short-staffed entertainment desk was not touched, largely due to Bunny. I heard on the grapevine that Bunny had put her foot down at anyone from her 'small' and 'hardworking' team being fired. We were grateful. Maybe we had been wrong about her.

After a point it seemed that the gutkha king had abandoned his plans to close EMTV, as firing more people without justification was quite difficult. The retrenchment drive stopped. Just like that.

Blooper

The tense period sealed my reputation in EMTV. I had a big fight with a big-shot reporter who accused me of 'crossing the line', 'not knowing my place' and 'being arrogant'.

That day was a perfectly 'safe' one for entertainment. I expected my 8.30 p.m. show to be dropped as it was a big day in the World Cup series—the semi-final between India and Pakistan. No entertainment show had any hope in hell against this particular blockbuster.

But at the last-minute editorial revamp, it was decided that entertainment could not be done away with altogether but should be preponed by three hours.

'Madam, aaj toh darshan jaldi honge.'

'Filmy masti-wasti thodi drop kar sakte hai, bhai!'

'Chiki!' I pounded her number on my cell, running across the floor. There was no time to lose.

Ever tried making a half-hour TV entertainment show in less than three hours? Don't.

Take a mercy leave. Take a jump. Faint. Tell them to take a hike. But don't let your editor lead you into that hellish space with an 'Arrey, you toh are a pro at it'. Bullshit. Unless you have a death wish. Then go right ahead.

Assemble footage from different states/shows/reporters, hunt for the lead story, write scripts and edit VTs of lazy reporters, you have to fill, fill, fill the run order... time is running out. There are no stories. So *get* new stories. Check ad breaks for durations, give the video IDs, get the video editor to start your edits, get the edit machines, but before that get the relevant footage ingested from archival, get the voice-overs and parallel dubbing of audio done, get the chats edited... by the way, if you are also the anchor, get your costume, your make-up and your smile in order—and did I mention the anchor links for each story? Get the supers in VIZ templates for each VT—a minimum of five supers per VT, so for nine VTs you end up putting forty-five supers, which means thinking up forty-five 'cracker' supers. And get the donut done, the shrieky little video that teases the jantaa repeatedly with 'Coming up...'

A nerve-racking, ball-breaking, back-shattering three-and-a-half hours later, I was too tired to even open my eyes when Martina dunked make-up on me. The thanda coffee only made it worse. I was dismayed when I entered the studio. My show's set had been taken apart completely. Our new channel panditji had predicted a sure victory of India over Pakistan if the set for the Indo-Pak sports special was shifted to where the *Filmy Masti* set stood.

Great. My set got shunted around, and now it had been taken away.

'No one will watch your show. Today, sports is big,' Bunny had called out when I left for the studio.

'Precisely my point. Why don't you make the fartheads drop entertainment today?'

Of course, the entertainment show did go on air. But only when the news desk finally decided that *they* needed a break from news and sports.

I was into my last segment.

'"I have given Shah Rukh Khan a break in Bollywood!" Juhi Chawla's statement…'

Two more stories, I told myself. Maybe I should call Rehan after the show was over. Maybe papa too. And I had to speak to Bunny about that Australia junket.

'All set to be cast in wax, Kareena Kapoor moves into the same neighbourhood as Big B, Ash, SRK and Hrithik…'

'Standby… we are crashing out!' the PCR director shrieked in my ear. 'Someone has been hit by a shoe at the Delhi presser, joota maara hai joota, joota… Laila, we will go to the shoe-throwing incident—get me the shots, patch to OB line three… where is Rene Chaddha? Shit…

'Laila, *continue* reading… we are going to crash till Rene takes over—Get Rene… *check the toilets*. What's the problem? Why is line three not patched in—every channel has the shots! You guys need to be more ready for this sort of shit—oye, did you find Rene? Kahan milee? Toilet mein?'

'… simply get Ranbir Kapoor to ask you out for dinner… considering that seems to be the ultimate meal ticket in Bollywood these days,' I continued reading on air.

'Laila, standby for a pre-rec of your links when we hit break. Standby PCR. Standby studio. Go Rene—'

'And in news just coming in… it was utter madness during the Delhi presser of… when a man tried to throw a shoe at the general secretary… things spun out of control… the assaulter has been identified as… the assaulter removed his shoe… a big black shoe… you can see the general secretary's stunned reaction… the assaulter was upset about…'

A good forty minutes later, the news desk was on the same news and the promised break did not happen. Rene kept announcing 'breaking news'.

'Hi, listen, who is the director, ya? What's the status—are you coming to me?' I was sure I had been forgotten in the breaking news insanity.

'Standby, Laila, we will come out any time. Be on standby.'

Still wired to the talkback and lapel, the backup radio mike stuffed in my back pocket, I waited.

'In what is now being seen as a security breach at what is generally considered to be the most secure zone in the capital… this is the third time a shoe has been hurled at political leaders in the last six months… a security cordon has now been put in place around the leader to prevent any repeat of the incident…'

I slumped on the wooden riser in the cold studio, my feet frozen from crouching, my fingers numb from clutching the hand-held cue gadget.

'… a touch to your left, Laila, and *do* fix your face. It has become too oily. Be ready to go on air in two minutes.'

By the time it was over, I was so tired I just about dragged myself to the desk. Like clockwork, Bunny dumped two back-to-back shoots on me and disappeared into her cabin to watch the match.

It just wasn't my day. And things were about to get worse. I don't know the exact sequence of things but I was brought to earth by some woman hollering. It was directed at me. And it wasn't Bunny.

'Who is yelling?'

A furious Rene Chaddha from the twenty-first floor was waving her finger at me maniacally. 'What the hell is this desk? What sort of people have been given a job? What the fuck are you doing not taking my call?'

'What are you doing on our floor?' I asked stupidly.

'I would not come to your chootiya floor if you bimbette cunts bothered to reply to emails or picked up your goddamm phones,' Rene hollered.

'Excuse me, stop screaming, I did not even know it was ringing,' I said.

'You have an excuse?' Rene blubbered, turning a shade redder. I don't think Rene had been spoken to like this by anyone. Ever.

'Excuse for what!' I yelled back and everyone froze. 'Why should I give an excuse for doing my work?' How could someone be so angry just because the phone had not been answered?

'You have crossed the line. Stupid little nosy twerp!'

Nosy?!!

And then it hit me. She had called me a nosy twerp. *A nosy twerp!* Oh god. Did she blame me for the toilet jokes? At Bunny's bidding I had unearthed unprintable details of Antim and Rene's toilet rendezvous. Soon the whole office had come to know, but not from me. Rene thought it was I who had told the others.

It wouldn't have been that bad if the whole floor had not come to a standstill. Neither by rank nor body of work nor physically was I any match for her—but I have always had very good vocal chords.

'You will be sorry,' Rene shouted.

'Girls... girls... *girls*,' Bunny yelled. 'What's happening, Laila? Don't you have a shoot to go to?'

'Exactly, please tell Rene that.'

'Rene, Rene! Darling,' Bunny tried to calm her down.

'Bunny, what the fuck is this, what sort of people do you have on your desk?' Rene vented.

'Shhhh... let's go into my cabin, why you bothering? Too small fry for you, Rene!'

'Small fry? Did she say small fry, that bitch?'

Bunny turned back and signalled for me to leave. I had been given a crash course in where entertainment reporters stood in the scheme of things in a news channel. Eyewitnesses swore they had never seen anyone mess with Rene. I guess it took a very brave person or a complete fool to cross that line. Not the way I wanted to be famous but the anecdote became part of blooper folklore. I was marked from then on, because inadvertently, in all my fights (and there would be many!) I was already pronounced guilty till I proved myself innocent.

'Tu hi kyun phansti hai? Why not anyone else?' Indu was surprised, and pretty pissed, that I still had a job.

'Of all the people you had to fight with, it had to be Rene?'
I could not believe Nandu had joined forces with Indu.

'Do you think she will get her ESOPs now? Rene is very
close to H. Raami and Bunny. She is way up, dude. Twenty-
first floor,' Chiki said.

They were still discussing my plight when I came back from
my shoot.

A miserable night followed a miserable day. With Rehan in
Africa, my sounding bag was gone. Shruti, my new PG, turned
out to be a very poor substitute. She slept halfway through my
rona dhona.

And it did not end there. I ended up stepping on some more
important toes. Despite my pledge not to get into any more
fights, I, within two days, had a public shouting match with
the head honcho of an important production house.

'Are you trying to set a record?' Bunny asked.

'Will it help if I say it wasn't my fault? He made me wait for
five hours, he was rude and…'

'There were fifty other media persons there—why was he
complaining only about you? Keep this up, Laila, and it could
get you into serious trouble.' Bunny had just read a long ranting
email, which the important production house head had shot to
her and H. Raami, complaining about the aggressive EMTV
reporter, yours truly.

'Look, let's talk when we have calmed down! It's a small
thing, Bunny,' I said.

'Oh, nothing happened, is that right? Let's go through the
list of your *small things*.'

Bunny started off, 'Urmila Bose from the censor board—she is so pissed off with you that she has refused to give an interview if you even go near her.'

'You know, Bunny, Urmila Bose is so stubbornly stupid. After working for decades in Hindi cinema she says she does not know Hindi!'

'You cannot force people to give bytes in your preferred language,' Bunny said.

'But why? How can I get Bengali or English bytes for a Hindi show? Bytes in fake accented English sound idiotic,' I said.

'But surely you have to think of a better way than "I am sure your Hindi is better than Shayan Munshi's"!' Bunny was furious.

'She said *that*! Like "better than Shayan Munshi's"?' Chiki looked at me with newfound respect. 'For once I agree with Laila—no one can understand her fake English accent after her son returned from abroad, ya,' Chiki continued.

'Oh, is that so, Chiki? So why don't you get that interview from Urmila now that she will not talk to Laila any more? And what about the time you introduced Esha Deol as Isha Koppikar on air and forgot Amrita Rao's name repeatedly while interviewing her?'

'Hey, the show still went well—you saw the TRP that day,' I said tiredly. 'And that production house chap… it does not matter to me. That chap can shoot off a hundred letters.'

'You know that chap is giving awards to eight EMTV reporters in his big TV award show. That chap is awarding three shows, including Nandu's, and two campaigns by EMTV. So what that chap thinks should matter to you. As it is, kitni mushkil se I got Rene to calm down. I am fed up of firefighting for you, and now this shit. What's the matter? I thought you had it in you… girl, you are falling apart!'

'Who is falling apart?' Nandu had just walked in.

'You heard?' asked Bunny.

'Ya, I heard,' said Nandu. 'But it's under control… I had a word with him.'

He had a *word* with him. I liked the way people always seemed to have a *word* about me. Right back to the time my dad had a *word* with my school principal when I pushed the princi's daughter during recess, or when my mother had a *word* with that bully Bittoo's furious mother when I hurled newly learnt F-letter invectives at him in a free-for-all. In fact, at age thirty, *I* should be the one having a *word* with someone…

I wished Rehan was here.

News 20-20

She had it coming. Indu, with huge chunky chips on her bony shoulders. Tight-mouthed Indu, who had the most maddening way of looking down at the little people—the interns, the trainees, the researchers—she even tried her eye assault thing with me, but let's just say she never tried it twice.

Indumati had been happiest when she was reporting large-scale fatalities and natural calamities, before she was moved (without a by-your-leave) to entertainment. Nothing less than reporting drought deaths or floods or flash fires could squeeze a smile out of her. She knew she did not fit here and had lately started hiding her face behind an oversized pair of glasses. She spent most of her time filling out forms for obscure awards and scholarships (and also managed to get quite a few) and this had made her smugness unbearable.

So when Indu was asked to report on the fun and fiesta of Bollywood Fashion Week, she freaked out.

'But Bunny, I only do serious entertainment. These fashion parties and all are not my thing. Surely you can get an intern… I know nothing about fashion,' Indu whined.

Bunny would have none of it. These were lean times. Editors across channels were balking at hiring fresh talent to pursue some Bollywood star for page three events. Newsrooms were being staffed for adequacy, not for specials and features. Like every channel, EMTV too was hell bent on retaining only as many people as it needed to bring out the next news bulletin. So Indu was stuck with us and she lost no opportunity to screw it up for the rest of us too. On the first day of the fashion week, Indu's eyes widened with shock when I turned up in stilettos, studio make-up, blow-dried hair and a noodle strap dress, in stark contrast to the bean bag kurta she was wearing. We made quite a pair.

Indu and I intended to keep to our separate ways but that was not to be. Reason number one: We had the same cameraperson. And that is the single biggest reason to start a clawing fight between two people.

The first day went by without incident and it was amusing to see Indu trotting around the glitzy venue in insanely drab outfits, trying to find human-interest stories. Nasty comments by sniggering hacks from other channels followed Indu everywhere, and I was left with the unpleasant task of defending her when they nicknamed her 'Grumpy Betty' and 'Dour Face'.

But today I had no time for Indu. It was going to be a busy day. The red carpet beckoned. The biggest stars of Bollywood were expected to walk the red carpet for the grand finale of the fashion week.

Latika was here, making her red-carpet debut. She had SMSed me to make sure EMTV was there to take her byte. She wanted to know if Bunny would be there and was thrilled when I told her that Bunny would indeed be physically present at the location.

We reached the venue hours before time, but all the good OB spots were already taken. Our OB truck managed to find a good spot but unfortunately the cables proved to be too short. I had no option but to depend on the camera assistant to double up as a runner between our spot and the OB van. His duty: get fresh tapes and go back with fresh feed between point A and point B.

'Aagey chalo, aagey chalo,' camerapersons wailed every time some lesser-known personality stepped on the red carpet. Barricades had come up on either side of it, and beefy security men kept a vigilant eye on the press. The first fight erupted in the first fifteen minutes.

'Bhaisaab, you are blocking my camera,' a reporter complained to a bouncer. 'Janaab, can you move to the right?'

The bouncer did not budge, and a group of camerapersons retaliated angrily.

'This is not the way to behave with the press.'

'If we leave, your event will not even take place. This event is for us, aap hatiye.'

'God, just look at their attitude… hello brother, we are not gate crashing. Hatiye!'

'Please madam, you are educated. Don't raise your voice,' the bouncer retorted.

'Hey, can you move from my cameraman's spot?'

'I am not budging an inch, babe. You check your position.'

'You will have to move. You are in front of our camera vision.'

'But why is your cameraman here? Rules say this is the reporters' area... one of you will have to go.'

'And who will make one of us go? You?'

Then the camerapersons decided to jump into the fight and it got louder and uglier. I felt bad for Indu, whom I had abandoned near the fashion-week stalls. Fifteen minutes into showtime I realized that my cameraperson had disappeared.

'Must have gone to the loo,' I muttered to myself, irritated with Arun for buggering off without informing me. After fifteen minutes, I called him, again... and again. My calls went unanswered.

'Arun... Arun!' The noise of a thousand people screaming simultaneously reduced my yell to a whisper. I started feeling the first panic attack of the night. Right before showtime, my 200-pound hulk of a cameraperson had mysteriously disappeared. I felt nauseous and alarming visions of a hysterical Bunny swam in front of my eyes. There was no option but to leg it and look for him. I tottered and stumbled over big camera bags, clutching the bulky gun mike in my hand. I must have caused quite a commotion because Bunny, who was enjoying a drink with her old cronies, noticed my graceless exit from the one place I was not supposed to leave.

My phone rang. 'Where the fuck are you going?' When I explained, Bunny yelled, 'What? Is this how you plan your shoots?' And then to someone else on the phone, 'Laila has managed to drive away the cameraperson.'

I felt my face burning.

'I don't care, Laila. You know the segment is sponsored? What am I gonna tell the sponsors? That my reporter *lost* her cameraman?'

'I am looking for him.'

At some point, I heard my expensive Gauri-Nainika dress rip. There were bruises on my arms and my make-up had started running. What I would have given for a simple pair of sneakers at that moment! Then I saw him. In the silk stalls section recording Indu's p-to-c.

'Arrey, it will take no time, Arun. Stop sweating, just one more take!' Indu, the hijacker of my cameraperson, said.

'Indu... Laila will be mad...'

'Oh god, let her sweat. She has made you sweat enough. She deserves it, ya!' I could not believe my ears. 'Just one more take and off you go, I have to file this story on the condition of silk farmers.'

'Arun!' He was wrong. I was more than mad. 'What the hell is this! Why aren't you on the red carpet? The stars are here!'

Arun stumbled about sheepishly, trying to collect his equipment.

'You run. I will get the camera stand, you *go*, get to your position.' It was the fastest I have seen a bulky man run.

'Shit... fuck,' I said as I bent down on all fours to fold the legs of the heavy iron camera stand he had left behind for me to pack.

'Excuse me! What did you say?'

'Shit. Fuck.'

'Did you just use abusive language?' Indu shrieked. Passers-by slowed down, sniffing a catfight.

'I didn't say shit and fuck to *you*. I said shit, fuck. But why this umbrage—you have actually tried your best to put me in a shitty situation. What kind of screwed reporter hijacks my cameraman before my show?'

'My show, my show! You know what? Your fans can watch five minutes of any episode and they wouldn't have missed anything. Your show requires no devotion, no attention, not morals or pretence or even an IQ!' Indu was seething.

'My show may be terrible, scripts over the top and maybe I wear too much make-up, but at least it's fucking being watched. You cannot fight the numbers—which you have never had.'

'You are crossing the line,' Indu hissed.

'What *line?* The cameraman is here for the main event, not for some side show conducted by you,' I said.

'You make the cameraman work like a dog, he was complaining about you,' she said.

'This is not merey baap ka video I am making! Indu, correct me if I am wrong, you have been filing human-interest stories for almost twelve to fifteen years, isn't it? Surprising that you have zero tolerance for humans in your own desk—'

'You will be in big trouble, just you wait,' Indu sputtered. 'EMTV never used to take people like you. Wait till you hear from H. Raami!'

'Take a chill pill, bitch.'

There. I had officially crossed the line, again. I knew Indu would lose no time in ratting to Bunny. I knew she would be shooting mails to all the important people. Bunny would be pissed as hell if she had to do any more damage control on my behalf. But I felt good. Seriously good, and hugely relieved.

The red carpet soon swam with superstars and their beaus and arm candy, the dapper Don Juans and dishy dilettantes, a long caravan of star mummies and papas doubling as chaperones. Expensive couture garments rubbed shoulders with diamante studded rip-offs, LBDs, desis, sharp sillouettes, ugly eyesores…

It was show time!

'Look who's tumbling in… kya pehna hai? Looks like a *razai*! If she could, she would probably wear the Jaipur jaali.' She was accompanied by a well-known face in Bollywood. She was the most-wanted on-screen mother today and he played father to countless superstars.

'Like Darby and Joan… he from his mushaira and she from her social cause… Gak! He should go easy on the cologne, dude.'

'Aa gayee walking fresco. Arrey, forget quotes, just get her shot, pan up and down her Kanjivaram and zoom in on that sindoor on her head, isska story ban jaayega.'

'Zoom in, zoom in… from that glitzy lamp behind her head, pan to her face. How manly she looks! I think she should lay off the body building.'

'Kafee maal milega aaj toh—ek hafte ka dose!'

Stars, big and small, were now arriving in hordes.

The comic hero, once fitter than a fiddle, today reduced to a puffy profile; twenty years of alcohol would do that to anyone.

Yesterday a comedy star, now he tried in vain to hook his audiences with stale jokes. The celebrated matinée looks were a thing of the past and he was a sorry sight with his failing memory and bloated face.

As for his companion, an eighties' heroine…

'Did she even comb her hair? Her idiotic films are flopping but does she need to subject us to this sight? How pitiful. I have a dossier on her stupidity.'

It was getting cold. What made matters worse was that the media was confined to an outdoor enclosure behind a massive rusty black barricade that seemed to be bursting at the seams because of the swelling crowd.

'Please maintain decorum,' Rachna from the event management agency yelled, clutching her bulky portable talkback that connected her to her headquarters. Rachna, whose job description included abundant schmoozing and downright chicanery, acted as a conduit to signal the important stars. 'I will be forced to call security,' she voiced threateningly.

Someone started laughing and a few people started making catcalls and Rachna scooted away to get 'extra help'. The bonhomie between the reporters and cameramen reached a crescendo. It was 'us' against 'them'.

'Man, check out that geisha and gigolo, you know these TV actors—look at that paint and gook she has splashed on herself.'

'Track kar… track kar! Can use her for the fashion disasters segment…'

'Oye, Sookhi is here! Take her, take her.'

This was meant for a top Bollywood heroine who had been losing pounds at the drop of a hat, her reed-thin figure automatically inducing a collective sucking in of stomachs.

'I lurrrve to be herrre,' she said in a dulcet tone and very fake accent.

'Can we get two minutes?'

'Ya, later, later.'

'You are looking lovely.' And then, 'My god itna bizarre accent maarti hai… where did she get her accent from?'

The star kid, the new poster girl of Bharatiya culture and sabhyata, made it to the red carpet with her entourage of mummy and papa.

'Ji namastey.'

'Mera fashion statement? No bikini, no kissing.'

'Ji shukriya.'

'Ji dhanyawaad.'

'Oh, lord! Will she touch our feet now?'

Shimmering in a black sari draped around her portly frame, the former heroine, one of the best at the peak of her career, walked in, mummy and daddy in tow, flashing her brown-sugar eyes.

'No LBDs for her, phir se Sabya pehna hai! When will she marry?'

'I am asking the shaadi question.'

'Then I am asking my question first before she gets pissed off with your shaadi question.'

'Why does a thirty-six-year-old woman need to hold her mummy's and papa's hands on the red carpet?'

'Maybe its vice versa. Maybe her mummy and papa need to hold her hand.'

'This happens only in India.'

'What's wrong with coming with mummy and papa? I think it's cute.'

'Okay, why don't you bring your mummy and papa to the shoot next time?'

Next came the actress who once had the most stunning face of Bollywood. She had been embroiled in a spate of affairs but alcohol abuse was what finally did her in—even her more-than-ample bosom couldn't help her. She had recently got married, but within a few days had started tweeting confusing messages related to her marital status.

'Arrey, yeh toh bahut buddhi hai; she is too zonked out from gulping down two bottles of bourbons a day. And I heard she takes tons of diet pills to stay in shape.'

There were intervals of tedious inactivity in between. The wait for big stars was punctured by a steady inflow of TV stars, models and designers. Big stars were followed by small ones, many of whose names I cannot recall. The entries were planned in such a way that every big star got adequate coverage. Tired hacks leaned on the barricade, some staring vacantly at the sponsor boards, others looking right through eager TV stars smiling extra brightly.

'Hi!' A TV actress stared greedily at my mike. I felt bad for her and ended up taking a byte, hoping she would finish before a proper star entered. But more TV actors trooped in just then, and made a beeline for me. I seemed to be drawing them like a magnet tonight.

'Listen, Arun, there's a bunch of TV actors coming in. I really don't want their bytes, but they are looking right at me. So I will ask rapid generic questions but *do not roll*—we will just pretend we are recording.'

The crowd erupted when the first family of Bollywood made its entry, dressed in different shades of black, their entourage consisting primarily of their favourite designers. Their PR agent announced grandly: 'Okay, guys. Listen up. Put your mikes together, you will get a group byte. Please limit your questions to the event.'

'That's for you, Aruna!' Everyone sniggered at Aruna from T Channel, known to waste everyone's time by taking 'Happy Diwali', 'Happy New Year' and 'Happy Mother's Day' bytes.

'I will ask *whatever* I want to ask… don't teach me how to do my job,' Aruna shot back.

'I hope he gives the byte in Hindi.'

'These days he gives bytes in Marathi too.'

'Hey, stop elbowing my camera stand. Stay in your position.'

Latika's entry caused quite a commotion. She came with the much-married Shyamu Sharma. But that didn't matter. The camera fell utterly in love with Latika. She was draped in a backless black gown that left nothing to the imagination. I had never seen Latika look this beautiful. Men gasped, women stared, and as for the shutterbugs, they couldn't get enough of her.

'You are being called Shyamu's new discovery?'

'I am. Shyamuji has been kind to offer me a small role in his film.'

'But what about Shabby? Isn't she doing the sexy item number? Why has Shyamu not given that to you?'

'Shabbyji is my senior. I respect her a lot. I want to learn from her.'

'Is that a new tattoo, Maya? What does it say?'

'Yes, it's some little thing I got done in… Shyamuji…'

The cacophony was maddening, making it difficult to hear anything clearly.

Shyamu Sharma suddenly stopped and kissed Latika on the cheek. There was a tense rustle and loud sighs amidst the clicks and flashes as the cameras went into action, and then reporters began shouting at the same time.

'Left… this side… look here…'

'Which designer do you wear?'

'I love to shop in London, New York and Paris,' Shyamuji replied as his adoring girlfriend looked on.

'He likes to shop for me from there—he knows what I like. I love getting gifts,' Latika cooed.

'Great! But since it's Bollywood Fashion Week, any Indian designer?'

'I love… you know, I can't take one person's name, they are all good!' And she sashayed away.

By the time the event was over, I was tired beyond belief. Lessons learnt: *Never* wear heels to any red-carpet event if you are on this side of the divide. *Never* lose sight of your cameraperson. *Never* stand next to a bouncer. It's the worst possible place to be even if you are a duly invited member of the national press. For them you are nobody. *Never* make a star, however small, think you don't want his byte. Trust me, he will never forget the slight, and it's a small world. *Always* roll a tape when the big stars are in the frame. Otherwise the big fat stories you miss will bite your arse later. *Never* leave your spot.

I had not eaten for over sixteen hours and though I felt dizzy and tired, I was not hungry. At the back of my mind was the unpleasant altercation I had had with Indu and now that the work was over, my anger erupted. I thought of the number of times she had created problems for me and how unforgiving she was to everyone's faults. My heart sank when I saw Bunny coming towards me determinedly. I did not have the energy to get into another altercation with anyone, least of all Bunny.

'Can I have a minute?' Bunny asked me to step out of the group of reporters.

Here it comes.

'So?'

'What can I say, Bunny, if you had seen Indu's behaviour—'

'Drop it, drop it. Forget it. Fabulous work, sweetie. You were right, I will not get as good a hack at double the price.' Bunny couldn't stop smiling.

'Really?'

'Also, I want you to drop that Latika thingie,' Bunny said.

'What? *Drop* Latika? But why?'

'I don't think we at EMTV promote tacky stuff. It's too downmarket. Leave it, okay. And that is not a request,' Bunny said before walking off.

So I dropped Lattoo from the run order. Clearly Bunny was not letting bygones be bygones where Latika was concerned.

In any case, what mattered was that I did not get a call from H. Raami, like Indu had threatened.

Rehan surprised me by sending me a beautiful scarf and flowers. It was not my birthday, it was the anniversary of the day he had proposed that we move in and I accepted. But what was he celebrating today—his freedom, or mine?

Drop the Bitch

'Shut up! You're kidding me! She didn't! She couldn't!
Did she really?'

'She totally did!'

'But her lips were lovely.'

'Shyamu probably likes them a little fuller, you know.'

'But the boobs too?'

Chiki had run into Latika at Shyamu Sharma's party in
Mumbai. Only, the EMTV hack Lattoo existed no more.
Latika had taken her transformation into Maya too seriously
… and got herself both a lip implant and a boob job.

'Shyamu had his arm around her and was introducing her
to everyone… She was wearing a sheer top,' Chiki screamed
in excitement over the phone.

'But how did Chiki land up at that party? Wasn't she
supposed to be in Goregaon shooting the item-number-special
series?' Indu said this so loudly that Bunny heard her from
her cabin.

Bunny had put Chiki in charge of the item-number-special series. The show had received superb ratings in the last two years. But this year, other channels had floated their own clones of the superhit show. The slot had been sold to sponsors but faced stiff competition and Bunny was under a lot of pressure to deliver the numbers. Actors, music directors and choreographers had been lined up in Mumbai and Bunny had laid out a long, tedious schedule for all of us.

Except, Chiki had other plans. Ambitious ones that did not involve completing Bunny's important assignment.

Bunny walked out of her cabin and snatched the phone. 'Is that Chiki? What the fuck is this? How bloody irresponsible. Where are you? Why aren't you taking my calls? What is the status of the shoot? Why… wh-*what*…? Bloody hell, who will do your work, madam?'

Being witness to only Bunny's side of the rant, we didn't know exactly what Chiki was saying but we caught the general drift.

'What the fuck, are we hiring journos or Bollywood wannabes?' Bunny was screaming at Chiki on the phone. 'Listen, I have a commitment, you jolly well finish your work. This is bloody unprofessional! I am warning you, Chiki, you will never work in a TV company again, *ever*! You can leave this company and go wherever you want to go. This, after I saved your arse so many times. Huh? *You* saved my arse? Girl, you have completely lost it.' Bunny hit the speaker key in her anger and we heard Chiki yelling on the other side.

'Saved my arse, yeah! Is that what you are telling yourself nowadays? That's nice, Bunny. Because you are the only one who believes it! You have used us to save your arse. I'm going to resign—'

'You are not resigning, babe, I am firing you and I have far more competent people than you on the desk. Giving you that assignment was a favour; the bosses wanted you out of this place but I fought for you... *you*!'

Bunny banged down the phone.

'What's with this desk?' Bunny looked around. 'Guys, if any of you are thinking of springing a Lattoo or Chiki on me, just be warned!'

She was in a foul mood. And H. Raami's latest mail, cced to the gutkha king, had made matters worse.

It's tragic, he had written. *EMTV's entertainment band is number thirteen this week. This is our worst performance. The reason I am sending this email out to everyone is because I think all of us should share this shame... I have just got the numbers and they are pitiful. Who is to blame?*

We avoided Bunny for the rest of the day. But avoiding Chiki's mother was another matter altogether.

Chiki's mother doted on her daughter and was heartbroken. She caught the first plane to Delhi when she heard that Chiki had gone off to Mumbai. White-faced and with her hair all over the place, she still managed to cut an imposing figure.

'But surely you have the address?' Chitra Bose demanded. 'What kind of colleagues are you?'

'Mrs Chitra, please. Your daughter is an adult,' Bunny said.

'No, something must have happened. She sounded unhappy whenever she spoke about this office, this desk!' Chitra Bose said accusingly.

'We can show you her mails. She is well. We would have an address to give you if Chiki had bothered to leave an address with us,' Bunny said.

But Chitra Bose was difficult to placate. She minced no words in blaming EMTV for filling her daughter's head with 'rubbish'. She blamed us, the desk, Chiki's so-called friends, for not stopping her daughter. Most of all, she blamed Bunny for destroying Chiki's peace of mind.

Chiki sent out an email that same night to everyone except Indu. Of course, Indu managed to get a copy by taking into confidence her friend in the IT department. Bunny forwarded Chiki's mail to her mother.

Chiki had met Amar Kapoor.

He was surprised to see me. He is a real man. You know, he is such a Shiv bhakt. He has given me a healing crystal and lots of good wishes. The mail ended with a cryptic *Can you please tell ma that I am safe? Not to worry too much. Tell dada I am having a ball; he should be happy for me.*

As usual Chiki left me open-mouthed. Had she jumped the gun? Had she been shortchanged? Had false promises been made to her? Was her infatuation one-sided? Chiki planned to stay on in Mumbai. She had Kapoor's 'good wishes'.

Lattoo gone. Chiki gone. It was just Nandu and Indu and me, and some interns who were expected any time now. I wished to god Bunny did not dump her item-number-special series on me.

I hated Chiki. She had bailed out and I had to do her incomplete work. Bunny was sending Nandu to get the Bollywood stars (she swore it would be a blue moon before she sent a starstruck woman hack to do Bollywood heroes). I had to go to Benaras.

'Benaras! What could possibly be happening in Benaras?' I asked.

'A Holi item number. Have fun,' Bunny ordered.

'Hey-llo, people… Guess who sent what!' Nandu's voice rang out. All of us turned to look at him.

'Oh my god! Latika's first-film first-look poster! It says, "Introducing Maya"!'

'Hey, that's nice! Maybe we can fit this in after the teaser in the second segment… Something like Shyamu's sexy Maya?' I suggested.

'Have you lost it?' Bunny roared.

'Sorry! You have something better in mind?' Nandu asked.

'Yes, I do. Just drop the bitch!'

On the Sets: Benaras

Nothing is sadder than a yellowing movie magazine

'Kuttiyon… theek se naacho!'

The snide remark from the dance choreographer got the garishly dressed extras moving. It was the first assignment for the item-number-special series, and my second day on the sets of a period film shot in an old palace on the banks of the Ganga in Benaras. The grand old haveli had been transformed into a Bollywood film set. The story was a sixteenth-century love triangle between a devadasi, a king and a slave.

A raunchy item number was being shot, with Holi as the theme.

'Ungli se khel, aankhon se khel, rangon se tu bahut khela, darling, ab mujhse khel…'

No one raised an eyebrow at the coarse lyrics, which had already been played over a hundred times. I was getting used to them. In fact, I had to stop myself from humming the obscene song. The choreographer's idea of a sixteenth-century item

number included heaving breasts such as those seen in Madhuri
Dixit's '*Dhak Dhak*' number from the film *Tezaab*, and butt
wriggling like Sridevi in her sexy '*Kaate nahi kat-tey*' bit from
Mr India. Twenty-five girls danced in front of the camera along
with twenty-five boys. An intimidating and robust woman with
a determined air bellowed instructions into a microphone. The
girls referred to her as 'Madame'.

'Madame rehearsal kara rahi hai... please wait,' a sleazy-
looking assistant director motioned us to a corner. 'And please
keep out of the camera vision,' he commanded. I braced myself
for the routine argument while Sandy, my cameraperson, kept
shooting. The third AD opened his mouth to say something,
then shut it and shrank behind a pillar.

'Oh gadhi Riddhi? What are you doing? You should leave
dancing! You have become too lazy... and *fat*! Laal shirt waale
ladke... abbey... what? Stay in line, bhonsdi ke.'

No one paid any heed to the expletives spewing out of
Madame's mouth.

'Madame ka style hai! She loves the girls very much, just
as she would love her own daughters! Boys too, unke bachhe
jaise hai,' interjected AD number two defensively. Madame's
sidekicks seemed to be coming out of the woodwork.

Madame's assistant gave her a hand-held fan while the girls
and boys sweated it out in the sun. 'Madame obviously believes
in wearing all her earnings!' Sandy observed.

'Come, come sit... Oye, get a chair', she ordered the AD as
she fingered the massive solitaires adorning her ears.

'First line, is this a comedy circus? Theek se naacho... kya,
khaa ke nahi aayee? Not eaten breakfast?' Madame's bottle-

blonde mop of unruly hair bobbed up and down with every word.

'Come here, tu kya kar rahi hai? Thakurji, girls ko breakfast nahi diya?' Madame bared her stained teeth.

'Amrita, iss ladki ko peechhe bhejo, send her back… Shruti, tu nahi seekhegi na? Monal ko aagey laao. Front! Ladke… oye boy, second line! *Second line!* Tu bhi comedy circus mein hai?'

Finally Madame turned to me. 'Sit down please, hello ji,' she addressed me. 'Get something for the EMTV girls… cold drink, you will have?' she asked. 'And you.' Madame turned to look at Sandy, probably trying to understand why a young girl with a pretty enough face was a cameraperson and lugged such a heavy camera around.

'Can you hold that? Very good… you are also well built,' she said as she made a gesture as if measuring Sandy's girth. 'You are too skinny.' She gave me a once-over.

I blushed. Sandy bristled. The paan-stained teeth with gold fillings smiled at me. I tried not to stare too much at the gold.

'You are shooting a Holi item number,' I said.

'It's not easy. You know these girls today, dance reality shows karke they think they have become Madhuri and Sridevi and Promila. Where is the nakhra, the adaa? They all want short cuts. But not in my dance, baba! I have to train these kids from the start!

'Hello, aakhri ladki… show me some style… thoda style se haath ghumao… I want patakas, haan!' Madame screamed into the loudspeaker. Sandy swore, yanking off the headphones and rubbing her ears.

'They want everything superfast... no patience, that dedication is not there! You don't become dancers only by going to reality shows!' Madame sighed. 'Promila was good at this, you know,' she muttered and proceeded to give a demonstration of adaas and nakhras. She rolled her eyes, which looked like a nakhra, and squinted and stared, I think, to demonstrate an adaa.

Promila Usgaonkar, the heroine of the film, was yet to make an entry. An unapproachable diva in her time, not much remained of her sexy profile and gorgeous body today. There was a time when you had to coerce her secretary to fix an interview months ahead. But post-2005, Promila's luck had plummeted. Her acting was over the top, her dialogue delivery buffoonish, her voluptuous body passé. She had been cruelly written off by trade pundits.

Life is hard for a heroine whose time is up, especially when she is past her prime. The phone calls diminish, the agent is always out of town, the friends no longer return calls, and the lovers disappear. Yet she waits incessantly for that one last film, the role that will change it all.

After a long absence Promila was gearing up for a comeback, doing what she did best.

Promi walked in with a diffident air, smile in place, and a curiously smooth forehead. Another jab? I wondered. She was surrounded by a prattle of PR persons and her secretary. Two assistants accompanied her, one holding her make-up kit, her umbrella and purse, the other holding a hand-held battery-operated fan and a big tiffin carrier. In a sheer white corset with a deep neckline, and something in white that resembled a dhoti, Promila was ready to give her shot.

'*Ungli se khel, aankhon se khel, rangon se tu bahut khela, darling, ab mujhse khel,*' the lyrics rang out and Promi, primed and ready, was hosed with water by the set boys. She broke into a very wet jig.

'Very good, Promi,' boomed Madame into the mike as Promi delivered her steps with finesse, and the crew and the group of junior artistes began clapping and whistling. Unnoticed by everyone, the second hero of the film, newcomer model-turned actor Sushant, had just entered. Sushant had nothing much to do in the film, less so in this dance number. This was an out and out Promi film.

The main hero of the film was superstar Munish Khanna. In his prime a golden god, today he was a balding hulk with a huge belly, unable to sleep, think or even string a sentence together without his favourite poison, alcohol. A good wig took care of the pate, but it was difficult to hide the paunch. Munish had been fitted into the song in a dream sequence.

'You see, while Promila is romancing Sushant,' Madame explained to me, 'Munish is fantasizing about Promi!'

The Amrapali-style costumes, the thunder thighs, loud make-up, the disco lights in a Holi setup between the big fat matkis... it was the eighties all over again. Munish Khanna was supposed to come running in and kick the matkis. Spot boys were practising firing giant colour pistols. Munish wanted to make a colourful entry. But where was he?

The film's producer rushed into the room with an assistant director. Apparently Munish wanted some changes in the lyrics, his gripe was that all the hot and raunchy lines had been given to Promi. Munish was now demanding that some bold lines be penned for him too.

'What rubbish… itne motey hai! Bhadda lagega!'

'But he is refusing to shoot till he gets some lines.'

'Arrey, de dey yaar! Do line dilwa de…' Madame said.

'Just give Sushant's lines to Munish too,' said the producer. 'I will talk to Sushant… it's easy, na!'

There was no easy way out. Munish Khanna's descent had started much after Promi's. But he had been hit harder. Dwindling film offers and cheating agents who couldn't care less had made him bitter. Munish's long-standing feud with his agent had led to plum projects going out of his hand. A spate of forgettable and mediocre films spelled doom for the stud of the late eighties and nineties. As the arc lights went off and the shutterbugs lost interest, Munish's temper tantrums only grew. He spent his days holed up in his vanity van.

But today Munish had had his say. Both he and Promi got drenched again and again in coloured water accompanied by scores of dancers making merry in the background to the bawdy lyrics. Madame had put in a lot of eye movements and flirty exchanges, wherein the girls tried to look coy and the boys cool, as they danced to the frenzied beats of dhol nagadas.

'This item will establish the love triangle.'

'Arrey, it's a challenge. Today, you have choreographers a dime a dozen. They do these reality shows but they have sold our bhartiyata… Dance is sadhana, it's a blessing from God.'

'Kitna culture maar rahi hai? Madame is very cultural!' Sandy whispered.

'What's your favourite Holi number? Holi ka anthem toh *Silsila* ka *"Rang Barse"* hai.' Madame stopped to stuff a juicy betel nut into her mouth, followed by a great deal of chomping. 'Abhi bhaang ka sequence bhi hai… you must see it.'

The tempo of the dance was not making Madame happy, so she volunteered to demonstrate the steps. Some high-intensity thumkas followed; she wanted more aggressive movements with the hands, fewer foot stomps, more chest pops and graceful arm swings.

'Keep an eye on that Promi, remember what she did in Delhi? Poora din she made the reporters wait, and then she disappeared, the bitch! Because it was a bad hair day,' whispered Sandy. 'Can you finish with her fast?'

'What do you take me for, a paparazzo?' I faked indignation.

'Oh, no. You will get the Pulitzer for the best item-number-special-series report!'

'Shut up!'

Promi's shoot was stopped as the owner of the haveli and his family were let in for their Bollywood moment. Munish's face broke into a smile when the girls started giggling and expressed their desire to be photographed with him. The men stared wide-eyed at Promi.

It was a curious twist. Heroines from top commercial films ended up playing second or third fiddle to heroes both on and off sets, while the exact opposite happened in B and C grade films, where women ruled.

'I will take a minute, haan…' Promi signalled to Munish, who nodded his head dismally.

'I am exhausted!' She flung back her well-coiffed hair and pouted her lips. The Holi colours on her hair glinted red and yellow. There was just a tiny dot of vermilion on her forehead, and lots of yellow—her most auspicious colour. Promi glanced at her reflection in the mirror held up by an assistant, and motioned to the make-up man to touch her up.

I felt like an intruder. But Promi did not seem to care. It was getting late, and I had spent almost the entire day on the sets waiting for her. But she was in no hurry. She was savouring her moment, making the hero, as well as the media, wait for her.

Life had come full circle for Promi.

'It gets easier with time or…?' I ventured an open-ended question, trying to get her attention.

'Things don't change,' Promi said in her heavily accented Mumbaiya English, 'it's just my ability to handle stress and all this sweat and grime that has changed.' She laughed and said something in Marathi to the unit hand holding her purse.

'You are looking a bit colourless. Why don't we put some colour on you?' Within seconds, dry red and yellow colours were sprayed on me.

'Now you are the rangeeli girl,' she said to the merriment of the set hands.

'No comparison with you. You are the original thumka queen, the rangeeli girl. You kind of introduced bindaasness to Bollywood dance.'

'Arrey baba, they are doing good work, hain, Munishji! What do you think of today's Sheilas and Munnis and the Chhannos and Chamelis?'

'But you are the original one…'

'Imitation is the best form of flattery, and I guess they are flattering me. My new item number will set a benchmark…'

'These days you have become quite selective with your film assignments.'

'I also plan to take out a DVD on my yoga sessions. And one on my fitness regime at the gym. I have called it *Promi Karegi Patli*. English version: *Push it with Promi*. Nice, na? What do you think, Munishji?'

'But your fans are missing you. You are only seen in item numbers now.'

'I have done my share of running around trees, and one gets tired of doing the same thing. You know, I have done so much cinema… been there, done that. I too want to play serious and meaningful roles, and I want people to see the actress in me, hain, Munishji?'

Munishji did not answer as he had left the room. I got to know later that he had once again locked himself up in his vanity van. Promi too left as Madame wanted her for a sequence. I did not get the miffed Munish or sulking Sushant, but who cared? I had got the interview with item girl Promi. That was sure to make Bunny happy.

There were some new additions on EMTV's entertainment desk—interns who didn't behave like interns. Especially Pinky Mehta. Not good-looking in the conventional sense but, as they say, expensively put together. She had a diamond-encrusted customised BlackBerry, and flashed her enhanced and accessorized iPod and iPad. She did a lot of Facebooking,

Tweeting and blogging. What was most intriguing was Bunny's 'being human' act in front of Pinky.

The puzzle of Pinky was explained by Nandu. Her brother's company was looking to invest in the cash-strapped entertainment shows. That she had been taken in at the salary given to correspondents caused much heartburn. No one ever saw her reporting, but her ambition was to be an anchor.

On the Sets: Jodhpur

Item bomb: a corrupt form of 'atom bomb', a slang used to refer to a sexy woman in a not-so-respectful fashion

The omelette was filled with dust. There was dust in the parantha, in the chutney and in the aloo curry. Worse, there was dust in the tea. The food inside the 'dust-proof' tiffin carrier was cloaked with dust. I was on my second assignment for Bunny's item-number-special series: Superstar Dandiya Nites. The superstars in question were Bollywood item girls.

I had covered half the distance between Delhi and Jodhpur. Six straight hours on the highway in a broken Indica, six more to go. The rickety vehicle was being pushed around like a toy on the bumpy roads. To make matters worse, my cameraman's snoring was driving me insane. I felt miserable. Nandu got to go to New York, Indu to Italy, and I was being sent to Jodhpur.

'Why are you complaining?' Bunny had demanded.

'Why am I the natural choice for such events?'

'So now you want to play high brow!'

'It's just that I seem to be doing only national shows.'

'What's your gripe?' Bunny interrupted in her lazy couldn't-care-less drawl. 'Nandu always does New York, that's his baby. And Indu's aunt is in Italy, so sending her there makes sense, saves the cost of hotels. And I can't think of anyone else who can do the items better. And if that new intern Pinky Mehta's Australia junket is your issue… yaar, she is a new kid, let her do something. You have to have a second guard ready.' Of course, she did not mention that Pinky came well-connected.

I reached Jodhpur's two-star Bharat Lodge covered in dust. The dismal and lonely lodge, masquerading as a three-star hotel, seemed quite unaffected by the commotion of the Superstar Dandiya Nites that had the rest of the city dancing to its tune.

'First they slash our salaries by 40 per cent… now this?' Arun snapped as we waited in the empty reception area.

The hotel finally swung into action when the manager appeared. 'Madam, me Ram Babu. So nice to have you here,' Ram Babu welcomed me to what was going to be my abode for the next two days. 'Madam, you come for Superstar Dandiya Nites? It is happening at Laal ground.' Ram Babu parted with this precious information in broken English. I urged him to reply in Hindi but he pursed his lips and continued in English, 'Madam, we have so many cars, very much available for transportation… You can have us any time.'

I told him I had my own car.

A group of men in the lobby stared at me suspiciously and kept nudging each other.

'... press wali hai...'

'... kahan se hai yeh madam?'

'... Dilli se, angrezi channel hai...'

I ignored the stares and avoided a few over-friendly handshakes.

I was given a chunky pair of steel keys to room 203 and routine advice to lock the door when we left, a quick reminder on the hotel not being responsible for any loss of jewellery, cash or equipment, followed by an equally quick suggestion to use the room 'safe' for our 'valuables'.

'... very safe, madam...'

'... madam, for food please call room service...'

'... madam, external calls chargeable...'

Arun was in 206, a reassuring two rooms away.

'Yeh deluxe hai? Where are the colours of Jodhpur? No way am I going to sleep on these damp green bedsheets.'

Arun muttered and sulked, refusing to touch the hotel linen. I could hear him holler for fresh towels. In my bathroom, a single sad faucet jutted out from the blue tiles.

'Arrey saala, there is no tub!' I wanted to strangle the scrooge sitting in production control for giving me a hotel without a tub. But entertainment shows meant less funds.

'Deal with it,' I could imagine Bunny yelling.

The situation would have been very different if Bunny's item-number-special series had been for one of those swanky lifestyle channels. They treated their reporters to 'first class' everything.

Their reporters did not travel in crappy cars. *Their* reporters were not sent to dark dismal hotels manned by sleazy Ram Babus. *Their* reporters always used bathrooms that had huge bathtubs.

I scanned the hotel walls, the ceiling, the lamps and the curtains for anything suspicious. Reporter or not, a girl's got to check for secret cameras in some hotels. And if there was ever a hotel that warranted a full body search, it was Bharat Lodge. 'Babe, check these sleaze-ball dens for hidden cameras before you undress. They may mistake you for an item girl and then toh… MMS Ragini nahi, MMS Laila Reporter will do the rounds.'

I took a bath in my undergarments and then ordered breakfast.

'Madam, American breakfast?'

'Please.'

'Madam, for one or two?'

'For one.'

'Sir is not with you?'

'No.'

'Madam, do you require anything else? We also—'

'No.'

I had packed a sexy silk top for my links but all I could think of now was stuffing it inside my suitcase. I settled for a pink kurta with funky mirror work and jeans.

Jodhpur's glittering Superstar Dandiya Nites was a platform where a mass-dating ritual of sorts took place. Unchaperoned boys and girls met and danced, potential grooms were sized up and future brides shortlisted. We reached the venue after dusk. It was an open area with huge tents placed at regular intervals in shades of vermilion and orange with turquoise durrees and multi-coloured wall hangings decorating their interiors. Table fans with water drizzlers had been placed to generously douse the guests in the hot night. The sky looked as if it had been lit by hundreds of colourful bulbs that twinkled like psychedelic lights. As the night progressed, the mata ki chowki songs gave way to disco beats, raunchy remixes and cabaret numbers. The crowd began to get restless as they waited for the three superstar attractions.

Thumkon ki rani, Shefali, Sherry, Reshmi ke sang, dandiya ke rang, the garish invite had said.

There was a lot of excitement about Shefali, a rage on the item numbers' scene following her raunchy '*Kaanta laga*' remix video where she had flashed her thong and managed to grab more than just eyeballs. From TV chat and stage shows to even a minuscule appearance with superstar Khiladi Kumar in a Bollywood film, Shefali had obviously achieved much more than she had set out to do. And even though film offers and TV serials had not materialized into anything concrete, her date diary was packed, as her roly-poly PR agent informed me.

'But aapka toh big channel hai… madam zaroor baat karengi,' he clarified.

There was utter confusion backstage. Junior artistes rushed around stumbling, tripping, half naked. Scarily, there was no security to shoo us out. They might as well have put up a 'Just walk in: item girls this way' sign! I shuddered to think what would happen if the mob outside were to get the same idea. Arun looked nervous, surrounded by so many women in different states of undress.

We walked across the length of the green room without being stopped, and were ushered inside a white door with the word 'Star' painted on it in bold red. Inside, Shefali was swaying to the raunchy, *'Mera jism jism, mera badan badan, main hoon taaza mutton mutton, aa chal… kholoon dil ke button button.'*

Bee-stung lips parted, she thrust out her newly acquired breasts, her hips gyrating provocatively. The smoking hot moves and jerky body movements left nothing to the imagination.

'Come in, come in,' invited the siren, who had literally brought the thong out of the drawers. Arun was right behind me, studiously avoiding looking at anything. Shefali had started swaying to another song. *'Kameeni tera bhoot chadh gaya rey…'*

'You do that *Filmy Masti* show, na? Mazedaar hai.'

I mustered a friendly smile.

'Can we take your cutaways, Shefali?'

'No, not yet. Make-up is half done. Take only my right profile, avoid close-ups… and what's your name?'

'Arun—'

'Arun, gandey shots mat lena!' Shefali warned him playfully. 'If you take dirty pictures I will come to your office and spank you!' Arun turned a deep shade of purple.

I left him with Shefali so I could do a recce of the area, and came across a bunch of young girls in shiny golden shorts and golden bustiers getting dunked in make-up. Some were trying on the assorted dresses, all made of some blingy gauze-like material, others were being made to wear thigh-high boots, chunky golden belts and garish golden jewellery.

'Imitation hai,' said a girl as she caught me staring at her neckpiece.

'Shefali is on, come!' Arun called out to me.

'First let's get these shots, with NATs up. Give me the sexy shots, the sweat, the grind,' I told him.

Arun focused on a group of girls in the corner who were gyrating to Mallika Sherawat's popular item number, a rage on the charts.

'Allah bachaaye meri jaan, ke Razia gundon mein phas gayee.'

'Behenchod! Return my money!'

Suddenly we heard angry shouts punctured by the choicest of abuses. Shefali was screaming at someone on the phone.

'I gave you the cash! Where is it… haraami, maadarchod, behenchod, tujhko katwaa dungi.' The tongue lashing continued for a while.

'Shefali madam ka husband problem de raha hai,' her agent told me. 'Case police mein hai, not a good man, that bastard.' Shefali and her husband, a small-time producer of B-grade Bhojpuri films, had fallen out over some money issue. He wanted a share of Shefali's earnings as alimony, following which Shefali had slapped dowry and domestic cruelty charges on him.

People, especially young men, were waiting with bated breath to see the gyrations of the goddess of lust. This was a time of suggestive lyrics. Tame dandiya numbers were definitely a thing of the past. Old favourites such as 'Aaj no chandaliyo', 'Kukdo bole' and 'Radha game ke game' had been replaced with raunchy numbers such as Yana's '*Babuji zara dheere chalo*', Meghna's '*Kaliyon ka chaman*', and Rakhi's '*Kamini tera bhoot*'. The first act, a live-wire performance by Reshmi, set the stage on fire. To the backdrop of the racy dance on stage, hundreds of boys and girls and men and women swayed to the racy number on stage. Women in colourful backless chaniya cholis and bandhni dupattas and men in beaded kurtas holding fancy wooden dandiya sticks with ghungroos attached to the ends created their own melody.

Reshmi, a popular TV bahu and a B-grade Bhojpuri film heroine, had no mean following. The crowd wanted her to dance to '*Sheila ki jawaani*'. Half an hour into the performance, Reshmi left the stage for Shefali's act, even as junior artistes ensured that the pace did not slacken.

My phone buzzed. It was papa.

Papa had not spoken to me since I refused to go to Africa with Rehan. We had these long gaps of no-communication at regular intervals. This was routinely followed by an even longer list of complaints about my profession, my show, my way of living and dressing. Before I was thirty, he was mostly anti-Rehan. After I turned thirty, he became pro-Rehan. In our last interaction, he blamed me for driving Rehan away. Several ugly exchanges later, I had slammed the phone down.

'Hi,' I said.

Silence on the other end. Until…

'Where are you? Some night club?' I could imagine papa wincing as he said those words.

'I am in Jodhpur for a special culture feature.' I avoided saying item-number-special series.

'Why can't you report news or business?'

'Papa, I'm not interested. Why are we arguing over this now?'

'It's crass. What you do, what your channel calls entertainment.'

'Papa, everyone does it.'

'Not everyone has done an MSc in physics. What a waste!'

I decided not to take the bait.

'It's very noisy. What exactly is your shoot like?' my father asked. (Just some item girls dancing in their underwear.)

'Papa, just something for the year-ender,' I said.

'Did Rehan call?' (Oh god, I hope he still wants to marry you.)

'Yes, papa, he did.' (Why is it that the only question you ask me is about Rehan? What about, how is your health/are you eating well/did you go on your foreign trip?)

'Let me tell you, he is a gem of a boy. You will not find anyone like him. Don't make your life hell. Don't go into the gutter. That's all I had to say. Bye.'

I kept my ear to the handset, listening to the disconnected call tone for a long time.

Outside, the crowd was screaming out Sherry Naidu's name, the main attraction tonight.

The night was cold, the air a dusty haze with all the foot thumping on the bare grounds, now to *Pal pal na maane Tinku jiya, haan Tinku jiya, ishq ka manjan ghise hai piya.*

My date with Superstar Dandiya Nites was over.

Chiki

Chiki was confused. Even after three months in Mumbai, all she had managed was one lousy meeting with Amar Kapoor. Of late, it was his secretary who answered his phone. Amar always seemed to be 'away'. So she tried to bulldoze her way into parties by flashing her EMTV calling card. But when she tried gate-crashing Amar's private bash she was unceremoniously shown the door. Of course, Amar never seemed to be around and pleaded ignorance when she managed to accost him at any press event.

But she never criticized Amar Kapoor in her mails. She never said a bad word about him. It was always:

He invited me to a pooja…

He insisted I go to his press conference…

He called me the day before yesterday and enquired about my health…

He said we must do something together…

But it had become obvious that Amar was treating her like a starstruck fan.

Someone said that Chiki's finances were a mess and she was borrowing money heavily.

'Her friends are avoiding her now, you know. She stays over on the pretext of visiting you and never leaves. And she has put on oodles of weight,' Nandu said.

'Must be hogging all day! Chalo, at least her face is busy while she is sitting and twiddling her thumbs.'

'That was bitchy, Indu! But then coming from you, why am I not surprised?' Nandu retorted.

'But where is Chiki staying, does anyone know?' I asked after making sure Bunny was out of earshot.

'She stays with some friends as long as they can accommodate her, and then she latches onto someone else.'

'But why isn't she coming back?'

'To do what? It's her ego, man! Big-time ego. And remember Bunny's warning?'

I remembered Bunny's final words to Chiki too well.

Forget about a job in TV ever again, Bunny had thundered. What I could not understand was why Latika was not helping her. It was obvious that while Chiki was floundering, Latika had landed on her feet.

But I had bigger things to worry about. It was that day of the year again.

Prime Time

'They are here! They are here! H. Raami has dispatched the green and yellow envelopes!' Mouli from the business desk shrieked.

I already knew. I had received the mail. *Dear Laila, please collect your appraisal from…*

I collected mine from H. Raami's secretary.

The yearly assessments were out. Some of us spent the entire year working towards it, some sprang into action from January. Of course, there was the formality of filling out the self-assessment form, thankfully all online and editable till the last minute. You were required to fill in the columns and the rows by grading yourself.

Rate your news reportage skills:

1. Outstanding 2. Excellent 3. Average 4. Below average

Rate your anchoring skills:

1. Outstanding 2. Excellent 3. Average 4. Below average

Rate your ability to work under pressure:

1. Outstanding 2. Excellent 3. Average 4. Below average

Ten per cent for skill, 25 for concentration, another 25 for being able to handle pressure. What about 100 per cent for being a general pain in the arse?

The grand total of all rewards was printed in the green and yellow envelope. One printed word summed up your contribution for the entire year.

What I was actually interested in was rockstar performers. If you were lucky enough to make it to the 'Rockstar Performers' list, you and your lucky friend got to go on a holiday to one of the choicest international holiday destinations. The topper of the rockstar list last year won a job offer in gutkha king's Mumbai masala factory for one of his qualified relatives. Lucky bugger.

The following individuals have through their hard work, commitment, etc., etc., made it to the etc., etc. Congratulations to the new rockstars! Have a rocking holiday…

Nope. As usual I had not made it to the rockstar list. The new rockstars were from the tapes library, some video editors, one production control girl, an engineer, a guy from graphics, two cameramen, some desk producers, and a reporter I had never even heard of.

Nandu decided to head to the pub with two editors; he needed a drink after he opened his appraisal envelope every time. Bunny's face did not let out much. But the moment Indu got her letter, she gasped and rushed out of the room.

'Must be rushing to H. Raami! Poor chap!' Nandu said as he left. With everyone running around for a safe spot to take the letters out of their envelopes, I went to the deserted entertainment desk and opened my letter.

Something about DA, some car fuel, ESOPs, car…

I read it again, my adrenalin shooting up. There was no mistake. Right in front of me, in printed letters, yes… *yes*! I had finally been given a car, with fuel and driver's salary, and 12,000 company shares to be divested over a period of three years! Finally…

I called Rehan. He disconnected the phone; he was probably in training or something. Or maybe not. He had not been taking my calls lately and sounded distant when I did manage to get through. 'Hello, he must be trying to figure out work in a new place, for god's sake,' Bunny reprimanded me each time she caught me moping.

I tried calling papa but hung up after the fifth ring.

I called him again from the car, but gave up after the tenth attempt.

Meanwhile, Indu had walked in and started typing on her keyboard with a grim face. What luck, I was bursting with excitement and wanted to tell people what my letter said, but, except Indu, I had no one to share it with. Chuck it. I plugged into the ISIS news software to make a log sheet of the raw footage for my next item-number-special-series story. I had edited Promi's item thingie with Ranjan, the best editor in EMTV, and the results showed. But Ranjan, though a genius, was compulsively obsessive (as geniuses are prone to be) about voice-over specific shots, and got really cranky if I did not give him the VO shots he wanted. This necessitated the scanning of each and every shot by me before his edit shift started.

Hell, I had all night. I had my ISIS news manager, my AVID newscutter and INEWS for company, didn't I? What the fuck was I so antsy about?

Nandu sent me an SMS. He had made it to senior associate editor.

Chiki sent a rambling email.

Hey, guys, how are you? I am getting by!

Please can someone go to my house and see my mom? Mumbai is a very strange city. Not like Delhi; here people are so matlabi! They don't give you bhaav if you don't know someone. Amar Kapoor has been out of the country for the last two months. I am going to complain to him about his rude secretary. Bitch! She told me not to call again! How dare that chit of a girl talk to me like that? Wait till Amar hears about this.

God! Too much shit for one night.

I crashed in front of the TV and watched *How to Lose Friends and Alienate People*, followed by *He Is Just Not That into You*, followed by *Kill Bill 2* and then *Intolerable Cruelty*, more than eight straight hours of glorious, gutsy, gory and gooey love—till my mind didn't have the energy to take in any love any more.

The phone beeped. It was Rehan. I disconnected his call. It felt good. So many people including Rehan had been disconnecting my calls lately.

Systems Failure

I woke up groggily to Rehan's call at 2.45 a.m.
Shit.

'What happened?' I asked, suddenly wide awake.

'Why aren't you taking my calls?'

'Like you took mine? Anyway, why are you calling now?' I
yawned.

'Dad had a heart attack.'

'What! Where is he?'

'Escorts Hospital.'

'Oh god! I am on my way.'

'I am already there. That's why I couldn't take your calls. I
was on the flight. I am here, in Delhi.'

'Wha... oh... where are you putting up?'

'I don't know. I came straight to the hospital from the
airport.'

'But you still have the house keys and your room is
empty.'

'You don't have to worry, it was a minor attack. He is doing fine now. Besides, visitors' time is over.' He paused. 'I have to go now.' I heard some woman calling out to him, and Rehan disconnected the call quickly.

I salvaged what was left of the night by looking at old photographs of Rehan and me in happier times. In most of the photographs, Rehan's hand was placed protectively around me, his eyes smiling. Then there was one of me with Rehan's sister Sheena and his dad. More than Sheena, it was Rehan's father who had made me feel welcome at their house. He often joked about how his wife had all the money, being from a well-known business family, and how he was just a glorified manager. The truth was that it was uncle's hard work and unorthodox ideas that had taken aunty's family business to dizzy heights. And he was the happiest when he got to know that his son had hooked up with a girl like me, and not some society airhead, as he put it. He made sure that I ate properly, getting their cook to make yummy fried prawns and that fabulous masala tea. He also made it a point to put in a word about me to papa; he knew I shared a strained relationship with him.

Rehan's mother was a different story. Icy and snobbish, she had thought I was a passing phase in Rehan's life and didn't understand how and why I had become a permanent fixture. And she disliked my job. With thinly veiled disgust she would look right through me at events where she, a member of the city glitterati, would be invited as a special guest, clad in her finery, while I, covered in sweat and grime, could be seen hobnobbing with the cameramen, balancing tripods, soiled scripts and p-to-cs.

Through not-so-subtle hints, she made it clear that I was not good enough for her son. Telling Rehan all the time to see the *truth*—that I was not the 'settling' type, that I was too career-minded to make it last; she even had a one-on-one meeting with me, which I never told Rehan about, when she tried to convince me that I was too different from Rehan and would never be content with him.

It was a tense affair. I was meeting Rehan after almost two months but it felt like a lifetime. He looked drained. His mother and aunts had formed a protective group around him, but I was here to meet uncle.

I entered the hospital room where he was. He held my hand for a long time.

'How is work?' This was invariably the first question anyone asked me, even a man recovering from a heart attack. Perhaps uncle too thought that work was all I cared about.

'Fine. How are you?'

'I am fine, Laila. Much better, actually. Loved giving the old buggers standing outside a scare!' His eyes twinkled and I smiled.

'Maybe you should lay off golf for a while.'

'How else would I meet your grumpy old man!' He wryly referred to papa. 'So how is Shah Rukh? And did Ranbir and Deepika really split? And is Salman getting married? How old is Salman now?'

'They are all doing pretty well, uncle. And Salman is old enough. He is still not married.' I smiled in spite of myself.

'Ha! The chap is old enough to know better!'

We did not talk about Rehan but about actors and films and Bunny and everyone else. When I left the room Rehan was not around. Sheena told me he had gone to get the hospital discharge papers in order. If Rehan was trying to avoid me, well, that was okay. I texted a terse goodbye message to Rehan, which I regretted instantly, but I was pissed that he was trying to make me feel guilty.

Glitch

'May I remind you that this is *not* a tits and butts channel?'

'What are you talking about?' I said.

'You need to tone down your stories,' Bunny said.

'Excuse me?'

'No nudes, no arses, no tits, no crotch shots, no chest heaving, no kissing, no bikinis, no raunchiness.'

Apparently there was a problem with my stories. They had been pronounced by some senior editors as unwatchable with family. Bunny had to slash the content. Bunny was furious— not with me this time, but she had no choice.

'But didn't you ask me to do an item-number special?'

'The shots in your last story were so raunchy that we got a show-cause notice from the Ministry of Broadcasting! H. Raami is furious. He has called me for a meeting where I will have to *again* defend your sorry arse.'

Gutkha king's aunt, after seeing the footage and stories filed

for the item-number-special series, was horrified at the 'alleged'
pornification of a news channel in the name of entertainment
and had complained to H. Raami. Not satisfied, auntyji was
now in Bunny's cabin for an emergency meeting—I could see a
lot of head shaking and outrage, interspersed with rolling eyes.
Snatches of conversation could be heard.

'… sleazy stuff *bahut* ho raha hai…'

'… but look at the TRP…'

'… we have too much naach gaana.'

'… you know the advertisers are happy.'

'… we want to restore the channel's dignified image…'

Of course, I had to re-edit some of the content, and my
item-number-special-series editor Ranjan was furious with the
extra work. But in a big way *my* stories were the biggest reason
for the hardcore family news channel breaking its rules. For
better or for worse, item girls had entered the drawing rooms
of the EMTV viewers at prime time.

I was on my last assignment for the item-number-special
series. I had to interview the self-proclaimed Marilyn Monroe
of Bollywood, Shabnoor Sheikh. It was obvious that 'sexy
Shabby', as she was called by her fans, had started believing her
own PR machine. Shabby had opted out of Bollywood after
the debacle of three of her Hindi films, but she did not head
south to Tollywood like most Bollywood rejects did. Instead,
she had headed towards Hollywood, where she had milkshakes
named after her, and had led the Indian Republic Day parades
as a marshal. She even starred in a B-grade Hollywood film
but it only managed a DVD release. She gave loud bytes in a
bizarre American drawl on how she hung out at parties with

'Salmaah Haayek' and how she loved 'Jawwnny Depp'. And now, after three years, Shabby had returned to give Bollywood another try. She was all Twitter-savvy and with a smart new blog space, and her Facebook account was full of pictures of herself with Hollywood stars.

The problem was that Bollywood did not give a damn. Shabby was pissed as hell that not only was Bollywood ungracious enough not to wait for her, it had also cheated her. The object of her ire was Shyamu Sharma. Shabby was spitting fire and venom at Shyamu, whom she had recently accused of attempting to molest her. She held a presser in every city. Today it was Delhi's turn. Bunny thought it would make a nice story for the item-number-special series.

Her real name was Salima Banu; she was a local beauty queen from a small tehsil in Ahmedabad, the only daughter of a lower middle-class conservative Muslim family. Salima, who had her heart set on escaping her middle-class dal-roti existence and a mundane marriage to a kirana shop owner, had come a long way. A new name, a new pair of breasts and a new nose had given her a head start. Shabnoor had erased all traces of her origin—her hair was dyed to a beautiful two-shade auburn, teeth capped though a bit toothy, big breasts and lips to match, a tiny waist and shapely legs. Men came on to her in hordes. On the net, Shabnoor's leaked item-number video that showed her gyrating seductively on the bonnet of a car had become a rage. Many said that Shabby had leaked it herself for the publicity. Intriguingly, the audience accepted Shabby with all her unsophisticated, almost rustic utterings.

Late by several hours for her own presser, she finally appeared, a vision of lust. Shabby's voluptuous body had been fitted into a crotch-skimming yellow dress, a barely-there yellow top, and five-inch-high shiny hooker heels.

It was common knowledge that Shabby had been excited about shooting an item number for Shyamu Sharma's new film. But Shyamu was reportedly unhappy with the shots and was re-shooting the entire song with a new and much younger girl. Sources claimed that Shyamu's production had convinced him that an ageing Shabby did not fit the bill. Shabby had had a massive face-off with Shyamu when she found out.

'He called me to his room… He was looking here… *here!*' She pointed at her breasts. The cameramen zoomed in.

'He said, take off your shirt. I want to see your waist… I told him what rubbish—main aakhir bharatiya naari hoon,' Shabnoor informed us self-righteously.

'He did not like me refusing him one bit. And then suddenly I found that I had been dropped from my own item number *"Baby Shabby"*. I had worked so hard—I left my Hollywood commitments to do this as a favour to Shyamu! Doodh mein makkhi ki tarah nikaal diya. But because I am from Hollywood, now I know girls don't have to be scared of these film-makers.'

She ranted and raved and threatened to take Shyamu Sharma to court. The media had a field day, the cameramen did not let Shabby out of their focus for even a second.

'I am a bharatiya naari… apni izzat ke liye main murder kar doongi!' Shabnoor wailed.

Shabby was not satisfied with just tearing Shyamu apart—
now her attention had turned to the 'sort of girl' who would
do anything for an item number!

'He told me he is keeping some new girl for this item!
Everyone knows who she is, why should I name her? Sab maaya
hai! Sab maaya ki kaaya ka kamaal hai. These young girls… Let
me tell you, he will use you and throw you. Shyamu can abuse
these desperate girls, but not me. I am a star.'

Watching Shabnoor doing her interviews was nothing short
of an elaborate theatrical. She was every TV channel's dream
come true. 'Shyamu, tum naamard ho, you are impotent,'
thundered Shabnoor. She was beeped and morphed, but she
was on all the channels *live*.

I was distracted by a call from Latika.

'Are you interviewing that slut Shabby?' Latika asked in a
matter-of-fact tone.

'Yes, Lattoo—er, Maya!'

'Did that whore say anything about me?'

'*You* are doing it—the famous item number?'

'Are you surprised? Babe, you should see my moves!'

'I can imagine. She called you Shyamu's keep.'

'Will you edit it?' She was unfazed.

'Well, I will beep out the gaalis.'

'Laila, I am just starting my career. I respect Shyamuji, but
I don't want people to see me as Shyamu's property, you know
what I mean? I have just auditioned for Vicky. But if it can
be worked out, the gaalis and all are so tacky, ya! But how is
Bunny?' Lattoo asked.

'Holding on. How's Chiki? She is in your city…'

'I know. Tell her mom to call her back. Chiki is making a fool of herself mooning over Amar Kapoor. She has totally psyched him, ya—he says agar kuch kar legi toh badnaam ho jaaoonga—Amar does not want negative publicity.'

'Can't you help her?' I asked.

'Babe, it's a different world here. How's Rehan?'

'He is okay,' I said in a small voice.

'Don't let go of him. Be a good girl, ya!'

Bunny was mighty pleased with the story. Of course, she did not let me edit out the part where Shabby was crudely abusing Maya. In fact, she wanted me to add my personal conversation with Latika-née-Maya post Shabby's accusations.

'Add graphics—a huge pic of Maya—and let the conversation text roll.'

'But it was privileged info, Bunny,' I said.

'Believe me, she will thank you. Publicity is good for these item girls! Just do it.'

Rehan did not return my calls. My texts went unanswered. But I had stopped feeling bad about it.

I don't know whether he could see my VTs in Nairobi. I tried to look more glamorous in my p-to-cs. I even wore my hair the way Rehan liked it. Would he switch channels if he saw me?

I became a morbid, sullen creature. I snapped at anyone who tried to be too friendly. On the offside, since I was so sarcastic, cynical and bitchy, my scripts became better than ever, according to Bunny. I felt no emotion. I just felt disconnected.

The vast grey blur of night edits fused into morning anchoring shifts—I had asked for night and morning shifts so that I could sleep all day. Where was the time to think about Rehan?

Love had passed me by. Only work remained.

Married and Published

'My ammi asked me, five-star ka khaana kaisa hota hai?'

'I was shocked. Kya, ammi? You have not had dinner in a five-star hotel? Maine Maurya phone ghumaaya... they said, sir aap! Please do come to our hotel, they begged me, but on one condition, you will not pay the bill!'

Waiting with the other presswalas at a shoot, I tried to ignore Sarookh, a former citizen journalist who had just been elevated to city reporter, as he launched on a monologue on Being Sarookh. In a short while, he had an eager group of listeners hooked onto his story.

'I told them, no! Gentlemen, if I eat at your hotel I will pay the bill. Ya Allah, I am not like that.' He rolled his eyes and looked skywards.

'Wah, Sarookh sir! Kya baat hai,' his fans sighed.

'Bas, ab GK mein kothi.'

'GK?'

'Yes, I want a place in Greater Kailash. Noida wala house I can sell any time—you know, GK mein I can buy a whole floor! But ammi says, Sarookh beta, ghar should be garden wala!'

Ughhhh! I couldn't take Sarookh and his ammiji's aspirations any more. Not that I could do much about it. I was stuck on a tree.

My mission: get footage of the secretly married top B-town heroine Sweety with cricketer Samrat.

As I peeped through the thick foliage of the tree on which I was perched, I wondered why Bunny had handpicked me for this particular shoot. How did I end up sitting on the branch of a tree on a busy south Delhi road, outside Samrat's haveli? Peering through a tree to get a view with a kill seemed more like the job of the paparazzi than a bonafide reporter in a respectable channel that prized solemnity in news coverage and looked down upon intrusive paparazzi-type reportage. Had I got the brief wrong? Was it a punishment assignment? Was I sending out the wrong signals? Was this the beginning of the end of my reporting career? Who would take me as a serious entertainment journalist after they saw me like this?

But the bitch was this: it had been my idea in the first place. After the roaring TRPs of the item-number-special series I wanted more. I suggested to Bunny that we do a series on India's sweethearts—stories around Bollywood love affairs. Bunny loved the idea and directed me to do the three most intriguing love affairs. And the first one fell in my lap when the newspaper headlines screamed that superstar Sweety, actor Niranjan's ex-girlfriend, had secretly tied the knot with ace cricketer Samrat.

Somehow I fit the bill. I was considered a natural peeping Tom. Oblivious to the open-mouthed stares and finger-pointing I was inviting from the general public, I renewed my journey up the tree. Planting my feet firmly on a stable vantage point, I scouted the venue for that one candid shot of the bride and groom. But the thick brambles cut off my vision. Far below, my cameraman was on his knees trying to manoeuvre the camera in front of the cracks in the compound wall surrounding the reception venue. It was a sunny evening and we were attracting curious stares.

'Look at that girl, mummy.' A little girl in a car stared.

'Is she mad?' a snotty boy next to the girl trilled.

'Press wali hai, beta.' There, papa had the perfect explanation.

'These media walas! Pests,' said mummy.

It would take much more than that to send me down the shame spiral.

Evil-looking security guards with angry guns outside Samrat's kothi kept us frozen in position for some time, till we realized that they were not really bothered with us. They must have been told not to throw us out, or the men would not have wasted a second in evicting us from our spot. Sweety's father did not turn up at the newlywed couple's do. Sources said he had announced that he would have nothing to do with his daughter after the wedding.

'Will you try for some bytes?'

'No one is going to say anything here… it's not Mumbai. That's why they chose Delhi, I think.'

'Did you get the shot? Anything at all?' Bunny called again.

'Not yet. There is no way in,' I said.

'Obviously, Laila! You are gatecrashing, remember?'

'I know. I will try not to get into any trouble—the security is no problem here; the issue is that there *is* no shot.'

'Man! I thought we were sending our most enterprising reporter! What happened to your can-do-anything spirit?'

'Ya, ya. But if I had known you would ask me to climb a tree today, I would have dressed appropriately.' So this was what the paparazzi felt like.

'Now the EMTV walas are also doing what we are doing!' Sunju, a veteran print photographer sitting on the neighbouring tree, remarked.

'No, no, this is a one-off,' I began defensively.

'You know, we are just paid photo walas,' Sunju said, his portly behind expertly balanced on a branch, hands clutching an expensive camera. 'I have this photo of a dusky heroine with that young, newly married minister at his farmhouse. Will you show it? I have a married actor caught in the act, pants down with a prostitute Who will publish it? I have stars stumbling out of rave parties and checking into rehab, etc., but the editors don't want all that!'

'Yehi chalta hai India mein! Thoda left, sir! Thoda right, madam! Very nice dress, very pretty tattoo, buteeful buteefuuul!' said his colleague Manoj from his perch on another tree.

Then I saw her. Sweety had never looked prettier.

Or maybe she had, about three years ago, when I met her for the first time under very different circumstances.

It was in a small studio in the outskirts of Delhi that I first met Sweety. She wasn't the size-zero diamond-dripping superstar diva of today, but a bottle blonde with the plumpest pout. I remember how excited Rehan was that I was meeting Sweety.

She was having a torrid affair with Niranjan—or 'naughty Nari', as he had been nicknamed by adoring female fans. I was assigned to cover the muhurat shot of a new rom-com starring her and Nari. The film's producers were excited at the thought of capturing on reel the real-life blossoming romance between the two young actors.

Rehan had made me swear I would keep texting him the 'hot details'.

Caught in the Delhi–Noida 6 p.m. traffic snarl, I was late by several hours for the film's muhurat at Noida's Jhaveri Studios. When I reached, a crowd of onlookers had collected outside the studio gates. The nervous guards, clearly not used to handling such huge crowds, had locked the gates from inside and extra security men had been summoned. Most of the TV crew was in and we were the last ones to reach the location. I found I was the only female in the swelling crowd of men.

'We're screwed,' I said.

'Walk very fast, don't stop, don't talk,' my cameraperson Sreenath said.

'Shit! You should have left it behind,' I said when Sreenath stumbled on his bulky tripod.

'I can't get steady shots without my tripod, and then we get nasty mails from your department.'

'Walk, for god's sake, just walk!'

We inched our way through the jamboree, which was a degree below officially 'out of control'. Sreenath cast nervous glances at the crowd and snarled at anyone who came too close to the PD camera and tripod stand worth over fourteen lakh rupees. I was more worried about my p-to-chip, worth eighty thousand rupees. We had just converted from tape to p-to-chip format and our shoot footage was now entirely digitized. My chip was dangling from Sreenath's front pocket and my heart was in my mouth at the thought of him misplacing it. The recent 40 per cent salary cut had left a bitter taste in my mouth—recession or not, penalty amounts had not been reduced, and there was no way I was going to cough up a hefty penalty for a lost chip.

'Let us in, we are from EMTV,' I yelled at the guard in my most commanding voice.

'Madam, yeh door closed… *not* open now.'

'This is idiotic, bhaiyya, apko camera-mike dikh raha hai—we are from TV.'

'Madamji, naaaa. Yeh toh nahi khulegaa,' he said.

'Naam kya hai tumhara?'

'Veer Singh.'

'Open the gate, Veer Singh, we…'

'Madam, aap andar baat kar lijiye…'

The clown wasn't about to listen to us. So I hurriedly pressed the numbers to connect with the PR, Harishji.

'Hello, where are you? You are slotted to go first, Laila,' Harishji said worriedly.

'I will come in, Harishji, if your bade saab at the gate lets me in!'

'Arrey, kya hua? Please give the gate-guard the phone.' A few words from Harishji and the guard's face crumpled. Six bulky security men kept the doors in place while a voice screeched, 'Madam, aaiye jaldi.' I tottered inside. The heavy gates closed behind us and Sreenath choked with relief. Inside, it was even more crowded. The place was packed with excited relatives and friends of the studio owners and an army of precocious kids. The stars were safely hidden behind closed doors, to be displayed at the auspicious moment.

The priest was putting finishing touches to the elaborate pooja thaalis laid out in front of him—each carried fragrant agarbattis, golden diyas, radiant marigolds. Also in each thali was a shiny brass tumbler containing holy water. This the priest would sprinkle on the clapboard, the exact site where the first shot between Sweety and Nari had been taken, as well as on the stars. There was some turmeric powder and uncooked rice, vermilion for tikas, the auspicious red chunni with golden gota work (on such occasions, red and gold were considered lucky colours), several coconuts waiting to be cracked, packets of besan ke laddoo and kaju ki barfi ordered specially for the muhurat. At that point they had no idea that the film would eventually be stalled, and released only after six long years.

We pushed through a sea of people and were led to some sort of secret ante-room, the temporary stop of the young lovers.

It was near impossible to get their complete attention.

He fumbled. She giggled. He hesitated. She sighed. He blushed. They had eyes only for each other. Was it play acting for the film, or was it the youngest love I had ever seen, as love should be… fresh, joyful, careless and fragrant. I felt like a voyeur.

'Hi, Nari… Hello, Sweety.'

'Hi,' said Nari.

'What are you going to ask?' Sweety asked a little shyly.

'About the film ya, what else?' Nari responded.

A nervous giggle.

'How does it feel to be working with Sweety?' I asked.

'How does it feel? Ha ha, it feels good!' Nari said.

'What has Sweety taught you?' I asked.

'Oh, she has taught me a number of things,' Nari said suggestively.

'Shut up, Nari!' Sweety blushed.

'So what has Nari learned from Sweety?' I probed.

'Well, how to act…'

'Is Sweety a good teacher?' I asked.

Some more blushing.

'What kind of co-star is Sweety?' I probed again.

'She is awesome,' Nari cooed.

'He is going to be a superstar, you mark my words.' She led, he followed. She teased, he blushed. Nari and Sweety weren't bothered by the uncomfortable surroundings or the curious stares. I left Nari blushing boyishly, Sweety with stars in her eyes.

Their film was the biggest turkey of the year. Everyone panned the young stars—their chemistry was thanda. Sweety was heartbroken and went into a shell, and it was only after her monster hit *Desi Dulhan* that she regained her confidence. Within two weeks came their second and last film together, *Love Ki Kahaani*, and it wove magic! No one had ever imagined *LKK* would become such a hit. Everything worked—the plot, the costumes, the set, the dialogue—Sweety had never looked more bewitching, Nari so compelling. The film went on to become a rom-com classic. But by then their love was over. She had become the bigger star; their relationship could not sustain her skyrocketing fame.

'Shot mil gaya?' Bunny's call interrupted my thoughts.

'Yes, Bunny! She is in a pink lehenga, looking pale but stunning, and Samrat is all protective and has an arm around her, and she is crying. I think she is probably feeling bad that her family is not here.'

'Save the poetry. What are you waiting for? Why aren't the shots here already? Nandu, change the headlines—pull out a story of Nari—'

'Which one should I get, the one where he has said that he is willing to work with Sweety again?' I could hear Nandu asking.

'No way! Get me shots of him looking grim, unshaven, eyes kind of red after a long bout of crying would be even better—get Laila's old chat with Nari and Sweety from the archives. Show me Nari pining for reconciliation and get me some diva shots of Sweety—glam shoots, all very sexed up—you know, bedard Sweety type.'

'What angle should we use?' I asked.

'Whatever sells the most, sweetie pie! Love, sex and dhokha, na?' Bunny said.

'But Bunny, it was not exactly like that…?'

'What are you complaining about? Your job is done. Sreenath got the million-dollar shot and you got all the glory!'

I wanted to text Rehan, to tell him I had met his goddess

Sweety today. I started writing with the familiar thumping of my heart; it took me an hour to string together a few simple words. I laboured over the choice of words—should I be casual or cool or emotional? How do I sign off? Love? Thanks? Regards?

I finally texted him clumsy details about how Sweety had secretly married Samrat. I didn't sign off.

I waited for hours for a reply that never came.

Keyed In

The mutton in the roll was tasteless. But I did not feel like fighting with Chiraunji from the office café.

'Stop pretending, start eating.' Bunny's voice was as sweet as ever.

'I am eating,' I said, and munched.

'You know, H. Raami is happy with *India's Sweethearts*. It is getting the numbers. But do tell what happened to your sweetheart? Did you get the boot?'

'Huh? What?' Bunny never failed to stump me.

'No, babe, I am not a snoop. What gave you away—apart from the fact that I don't see Rehan's car hanging around here—is that you don't smile except when you are on air.'

'What rubbish!' I tried a smile.

'Babe, don't give me that fake on-air smile. So, were you stupid enough to give him the boot, or was he smart enough to give you one?'

'You know I am...'

'You look scared.'

'For your information, Bunny, I am in a special space. I am very very fine. Just sort of shaky and incredibly lonely and madly numb. But otherwise I am fine. Thank you.'

'What did he do? Two-timed you? I'm not surprised. Don't feel bad, it happens to the best…'

'Rehan did not two-time me!'

'It's okay to talk, sweetie. What did he do? Did not want to marry a TV reporter? Turned out to be mamma's boy? Asked you to leave your job? Hit you? Took your money?'

'No! Nothing so dramatic,' I said numbly. Bunny smiled and shrugged her shoulders. Of course she was right.

I had been stupid.

Rendering Error

She was embarrassed that she had declared her love for Subeer Sinha publicly. She was taken aback by the incessant scrutiny of her relationship with Subeer. The media's rabid obsession with her 'SS' voice-mail greeting in three different languages shook her. Why did she alone have to bear the brunt of the media attack, Sheila lamented to her friends. How did her two-timing former lover go scotfree? Did she consider voice-mail to be the biggest mistake of her life?

Looking pale and stressed and distracted, it was a very different Sheila Dabke at the presser, a far cry from the fresh-faced Shelly I used to run into during fashion weeks when she was an upcoming model, a tall stunner with happy, frank eyes and a graceful smile.

At her first presser after her breakup, she made feeble attempts to smile. She fingered her chignon nervously and the distress in the doe-like eyes was apparent. For the media hounds she was fair game.

'She has become too thin.'

'Stick, man, sookhi lakdi.'

'Smile bhi fake hai.'

'Poor kid…'

'She looks so lost… like a waif.'

'She is dignified, ya.'

'That she is, but boring, you know what I mean?'

'It was bound to happen. How can you be so naïve about Bollywood actors, that too Subeer?'

'Well, she is better off without him!'

'Oye, he is not holding his breath for her.'

'She has learned the hard way, poor thing.'

'If she has learnt at all, that is!'

The breakup between Bollywood's youngest sweethearts Sheila and Subeer was big news for entertainment reporters.

What everyone wanted to know was what had gone so wrong in the most celebrated love story?

She, a supermodel-turned actress, had been on a high after her monster debut hit *Sajna Anaadi Beimaan*. He was on a roll after his superhit debut *Khiladi Main Bhi*.

Off screen, the moment they laid eyes on each other, the sparks flew. They were often spotted at glittering parties and film premieres, lost in each other. The media went on about how Subeer was utterly in love with the fresh-faced Sheila, how she had snared the most eligible bachelor in town, how a rank outsider had hijacked Subeer away from the tinsel town hotties. Overnight she became Bollywood's most envied actress.

Then she threw caution to the winds and came out with the tell-all voice-mail. A week later, reports doing a postmortem on the most celebrated love affair surfaced. Truth was that Subeer was ready to move on. He started giving bytes on television.

'I am just twenty-eight, ya…'

'I have not found my soul mate yet…'

'I have had three relationships so far but not one was serious…'

Subeer was already referring to the relationship with her as something in the past. And the most telling of all remarks: 'Sheila is a good girl… she will get married soon…'

I was jolted back to the present with Saryu asking Sheila cheekily, 'You have broken up with Subeer, so why do you still have the tattoo?'

'I have made bad choices,' Sheila said quietly. 'This will remind me of my mistakes.' At that moment there wasn't a single person who didn't feel sorry for her.

Subeer's casual remarks must have hurt like hell, and they were looped and shown again and again on every channel. Sheila had discovered the true nature of the media. That too must have hurt.

'I have great respect for him as a friend. He is a great actor.'

'What about your joint endorsement of that new aphrodisiac? Is that off now?'

'I am too busy with my films.'

'What do you think Subeer should endorse?'

'Nothing, really.'

But just before she gracefully got up to leave, she added softly, 'Maybe he should endorse Shilajit.'

I missed it at first. But the press erupted in laughter. I could see the headlines—'Sheila ki jeet!'

Subeer's ex-sweetheart had just turned the press, which had built and then torn her down so mercilessly, into her personal weapon of destruction. India's sweetheart had arrived.

I felt like my heart would burst.

I reached home at night, dead tired from the item-number-special-series edit. There was a moment when I could have stopped the dam from bursting, but then I thought, how bad could it be?

And then it just burst. After twenty-eight days of Rehan leaving for Africa, I felt my air whoosh out. Fear hit me in the face—had I been ditched for good? It was not just that Rehan was perfect and made me feel safe, but it had been as easy as breathing with him. Was I too dysfunctional for the normal thing? I had heard that seven years was all it took for your body cells to regenerate completely, to effectively make you a new person. So had I mutated somewhere inside? Because it wasn't supposed to be this way.

I had ditched him too many times, but a part of me always thought he would understand. Not long ago, all I wanted was to be the kind of girl he wanted… but I had turned out like this.

Had I been running away from reality for too long? I had to face the truth. Rehan did not want anything to do with the sort of person I had become.

I cried for hours.

Chiki called, but I did not feel like talking to her. I did not want to talk about love, period. Chiki had been sending me bizarre mails, and I suspected she needed someone to vent to but I was too depressed.

Was there a nice way to tell someone to lay off? In any case, all Chiki was ever interested in was knowing what was happening with Bunny, with Nandu, with Indu and with me. She refused to reveal anything about her life in Mumbai. Whenever I tried to ask her what was happening between Amar and her she clammed up. And she refused to talk about Maya.

The phone stopped after the sixth ring.

On Air

'How is it your business? Oye, Millimetre? I am talking to you. And why ask me? Ask Sweena!' Superstar Czar Oberoi's eyes bulged out of his sockets as he berated the hapless pint-sized Gogol.

Gogol's crime: he had asked the wrong question.

The blood-red flecks in Czar's eyes stood out prominently, his ears flattened and his body wired up tightly, ready to lash out. His eyes looked feral from lack of sleep (two hours was the maximum he was getting!).

'Arsehole! He is deliberately trying to intimidate the media,' Gogol hissed.

Czar had dislodged the bulky table mike from its stand and was swinging it maniacally—as if he wanted to fling it at someone. Everyone waited for someone else to ask the questions they had come to ask. The media wanted to know why Czar had not turned up at his on-and-off girlfriend Sweena Patel's production house launch party. She had, after all, declared him the guest of honour. She had also bombarded the media with invitation cards that had Czar's name all over them. Sweena had made the media wait past midnight, hoping he would deliver on his promise.

But even after ditching her shamelessly, Czar was unapologetic.

At the presser for his film, he rolled up his sleeves, flexed his ample muscles and glared at anyone daring to ask a question about Sweena Patel. In fact, he was hopping mad that the media was asking too many personal questions and intruding on his private life. And when Saryu asked him why he skipped the party, he erupted.

'Are you married?' Czar asked.

'No,' Saryu said.

'Boyfriend toh hoga?' Czar persisted.

'Yes,' Saryu said.

'Uske saath bhi reporteri karti ho? You ask your boyfriend such questions—*where* were you? With *whom*? *Why*? *For how long*?' Czar screamed at a stunned Saryu.

'It was just a question,' Saryu muttered.

Shit. The PC was effectively over. Saryu refused to ask further questions…

But Gogol was not too disappointed.

'That's the story. Czar got abusive at the mention of Sweena's name!'

It had started with Czar's casual comment to a reporter who was quizzing him on his relationship status with sexy Sweena. 'Sweethearts can evolve in different ways…'

'I want all the murky details,' Bunny had insisted before

I left for Czar's live presser. That I was not exactly Czar's 3 a.m. friend, she conveniently ignored.

Czar was not interested in giving any clarification on his love life. Naturally, Czar's behaviour was presented, distorted and twisted by the media in every way possible. Everyone wanted a piece of the Czar-Sweena breakup pie. Channels started dishing out facts and half truths on the state of their relationship.

The story was moving faster than we could follow. Especially when the media acted as messenger and dutifully delivered Czar's relationship status to Sweena at a fund-raising event. For poor Sweena there was no escape from the avalanche of questions:

'Are you two splitting up?'

'Get her expression, give me a close up.'

'Aap dono alag ho gaye hai? Have you two separated?'

'Zoom into her eyes—pan down, pan down—get her clenched fingers.'

'Kaisa lag raha hai? How are you feeling?'

'Are you breaking up with him or has he broken up with you?'

'If she cries I want that, so stay very close.'

'Czar says he is single… and you?'

A flabbergasted Sweena blurted out, 'Well, if Czar says so, who am I to say we are together? If he is single, well, I am single too.'

Was there a catch in her throat? Did she stumble?

'Shit, didn't she cry?'

'Arrey, freeze her shot and change colour… Bijli maar dena peechhe se.'

'I will create false tears and place them on her cheeks.'

She may not have cried, but Sweena had just complicated matters by officially giving a statement to the media confirming that she was not with Czar any more.

Members of the press faithfully conveyed Sweena's reaction to Czar, who went berserk at the live presser. After all, no one *left* Czar. Not even as a joke. Bunny wanted me to prod him with provoking questions during the media interaction. That's the best way to reveal his shitty act, she said.

'Woh kehti hai toh okay! But kal raat tak toh nahi thhe! We were together last night too,' Czar taunted and his feed went out live to his fans. 'She and I are together, at least we were till last night! But when will Millimetre here understand?'

'But Sweena threw a party just for you,' I shouted into the mike. 'You ditched her, Rehan, obviously that means nothing to you. She is there for you… what about you being there for her? We have heard that she is trying to contact you but—'

Suddenly it hit me that I had blurted out Rehan's name in place of Czar's. Faced with the confused stares of the media and the superstar, I hurried to rectify the situation… but it was too late.

'Naam toh theek le lo yaar.' Czar was miffed that a reporter had forgotten his name in a live presser. There was no way to edit that out now.

'Sorry, I didn't mean to,' I stammered.

But Czar was not about to let go that easily.

'You can't even get the name right, what business is it of yours that you ask me such questions?'

Shit. It was my turn in Czar's doghouse today.

'I am sor—'

'You, press walis, you crucify us for one look, but madam, what do I say to you?'

Nothing, *please*.

'Today you call me Rehan. Tomorrow you will call me Ronny. Then you will say Ronny is going out with Sweena. You guys create news in this way? Shhh, listen… shhh… there is "hot" news… filmy-vilmy masti… movie-shovie masala?'

All this was *live*. Shut up, please. I stared fixedly at a point on the curtain behind Czar.

'Sorry, Czar! I meant, what is your relationship status?'

'Yesterday, it was committed. Today, it is complicated. About tomorrow, I will know tomorrow night. I hope you will remember my name now.' Czar's cheeky reply got quite a few claps. But I was finding it hard to concentrate.

Rehan… shit. *Shit*. Why did I have to take Rehan's name?

The *India's Sweethearts* series got fantastic numbers.

'Even the repeats are touching twenty–twenty-five.' Bunny was ecstatic.

I turned pale and became teary, and we both pretended it was for the good copy.

After the item-number-special series, this was the best thing to have hit the channel in entertainment and Bunny was mad with excitement. H. Raami was pleased, and sent a congratulatory mail, copying in the gutkha king.

Nandu had been given a new campaign. Indu was working on a new special on Bollywood junior artistes.

And Bunny promised me a juicy foreign junket. But I had had enough of specials.

I requested Bunny for a change in pace to deal with my brain, which had stopped working.

Boring Story

'How many ways will I report Raaja Babu and Ronsher? Buggers get five crore every time I get my measly two-minute VT on air with a hundred riders,' I whined to Bunny.

I was pissed off with life in general.

'Do the fashion week or the art show, or maybe some page three scene? Or some good causes such as charity events for the girl child or the disabled or something on the environment,' Bunny suggested, handing me a few colourful invites.

'It's all for a good cause,' said actor Faheen Khan, a practised smile plastered on his puffy face.

'Dude, his filmy career is so over.'

'What to ask?'

'I should ask him about the bust-up at this Mumbai night club where he was caught snorting his favourite poison in the loo, or the very public fight he had with that Dilli designer!'

'Poochh, poochh, na!'

'What a thakela event!'

A product endorsement had brought Faheen Khan to Delhi; the out-of-work actor struck a tested pose—always his right profile—for the shutterbugs. It was the launch of the Chawla Boutique in Delhi's South Extension area.

The beaming daughters of the store owner in their Gauri-Nainika creations got to sit with Faheen for a full forty-five minutes.

'I think they want to stuff and hang him up like a trophy!'

'What a lovely idea. Maybe that's the only way we will be spared of Faheen's Bollywood misadventures!'

Chawlaji was the father of twin daughters who became fashion designers on their twentieth birthday. The boutique was a gift from papa.

Soon I was off to another good cause, a fundraiser held in the capital in aid of physically challenged athletes. There would be high spirits and lots of Som Tam and vermicelli salad. The main course included Kapraw Tow Hu, Paad Thai, Bangkok Fish and Star of Siam. There were live performances by a very excited Kolkata singer and a non-committal Sufi singer. The city's cocktail set was out in their Varun Bahls and Monica Jaisinghs, all very earnest about contributing to a worthy cause.

Then there was an event against drunken driving at the Grand Intercontinental's Blue Elephant. There was lavish, mouthwatering Japanese cuisine to tickle the palate and performances by an exotic dance troupe specially flown in from Europe. Delhi's champagne set, the embassy walas, a smattering of artistes and the ubiquitous page three types were present at the event.

The bash at the swanky F Bar was the talk of the town. Delightful live creatures were jumping out of gargantuan cakes and girls were waltzing around in bunny costumes. The bar was built on one floor that was split into two, with small digital TVs perched on oblong tabletops and in the Long Island bar lounges.

DJ Ali, specially flown in from Mumbai, belted out rhumba, samba, salsa, tango and Latino numbers. It was a setting for the preview of an all-male spring-summer collection by designer Sidharth Tuteja, the only son of a minister of the ruling party. The models mingled with the crowd so one could see the clothes properly and even touch the material.

'I want my men to break out of the stereotype. I want my men to show some skin. I want my boys real pretty,' the sozzled designer said.

It was at this precise moment that Bunny's SMS came. Chiki was home. And she had slashed her wrists. Her mother had found her in the toilet.

Kill It

I will never forget the sight of Bunny pulling out Chiki's nearly lifeless body from her mother's arms. The gush from the mangled hands had reduced to an ooze by the time Bunny reached Chiki's residence with a doctor. God knows why Mrs Bose called Bunny instead of an ambulance, but perhaps that was what saved Chiki's life. Bunny had the presence of mind and the contacts to summon an efficient doctor just a few blocks away from her house. I shudder to think what Chiki's fate would have been if her hysterical mother had driven her all by herself to the hospital. After a few hours, the doctor said she would be fine but had to stay in the hospital for a few days.

The meat cleaver with which Chiki had proceeded to carve herself was blunt and that's what saved her life.

Wasn't it enough that she would survive? But I was bubbling with impotent fury. Not so much at Amar Kapoor, who led Chiki to believe in him, and dumped her to fend for herself.

Nor at Latika, who could have helped but didn't. Not even at Indu who mocked her, or Bunny who fired her from EMTV. I was mad at myself, for I was the one she had been calling every day for succour. When did I stop paying attention to a real cry for help? Chiki, the woman with 840 Facebook connections, had no friend to turn to when push finally came to shove. Her friends abandoned her. I had disconnected her last call. Her last SMS, which I had not even bothered to reply to, just said, *Nice show*.

And before that she had texted me a line from her favourite song: '*This used to be a fun town but now it is full of evil clowns…*'

I was ashamed. I had not asked a single question at the one place where I was supposed to. Why, *why* didn't I ask the questions? Why did I ignore the one terrible truth playing out in front of me?

'She will survive,' said Bunny wearily as she came out of the hospital room. I had never seen Bunny so devastated. In those desperate hours, Bunny had revealed herself as someone who was humane. For now, Chiki would survive. But whether she would recover or not was the bigger question.

Aligned

I refused to go back to active mainstream Bollywood reporting for some time, so Bunny continued handing me the 'good causes'. I didn't mind covering them, really.

It was late at night when I went home from the hospital, where I was spending a lot of time with Chiki after the shoots.

Standing inside my apartment, I took a long time to decide whether I should go for Cuppa Noodles or ginger tea. Finally, I took a shower instead.

After that I plonked down on my Fatboy two-seater and gorged on some good old-fashioned starch—macaroni-cheese and garlic bread—that's the only way I was getting any sleep. Slumped into a drugged state induced by the carbs, I fumbled for the remote.

'Looking for this?'

I froze.

'So, what happened to the sweethearts?'

I remained frozen.

'I was waiting for your SMS.'

I did not turn. I just wanted to hold onto the moment.

'You have become skinny. Your eyes bulge out of your sockets during your p-to-cs. Aren't they putting any make-up on you, Skeletor? And let's not even talk about your hair. It's alarming what EMTV will put on air nowadays! I had to rush back. I don't want to be responsible for your total collapse.'

'Shut up, fucker. Who is collapsing? I'm doing fine, but Chiki—'

'I heard. We all make mistakes.'

'Yes, Rehan. We all do.' I held my breath.

'But yours was inexcusable, Laila. Mistaking that obnoxious Czar for me? At a live presser! Now that moment is eternalized. What were you thinking?' He smiled, and I exhaled.

'That was an honest mistake. Haven't you ever made one?'

'Okay, I will tell you the truth.' Rehan raised his hand and placed it on his chest in a dramatic gesture. 'I did make a mistake. And then I realized. The change occurred after your increment. I got your SMS about your ESOPs and car, and I thought to myself,' Rehan rolled his eyes, 'I thought to myself, what the heck! I have this incredibly rich woman working like a bitch, so I thought I must ask you that one question—will you let me be your dog some more?'

'Only if you lick my feet, mutant!'

'Just a warning. If I stay here tonight it will mark the beginning of something you will not be allowed to run from any more.'

'Who has been running from whom?' I asked. We held each other for a long time without saying a word.

'You look like a ghost,' Rehan said. I thought I would let him have the final word for once.

'By the way, Rehan, you were wrong about Bunny.' Then again, maybe not.

Hard Copy

> *You cannot hope to bribe or twist, thank god, the British journalist, but seeing what the man would do unbribed, there's no occasion to.*
>
> — HUMBERT WOLFE, BRITISH JOURNALIST

> *They may not British be, but Mr Wolfe, in matters of impropriety and thievery, the Indian journalist too, I promise, will not disappoint thee.*
>
> — ANONYMOUS

'Laila, you are not sounding at all well today, darling. Take the day off. Nandu will handle your edits, sweetie.'

'No, Bunny, I'm fine. Actually, I am feeling much better.'

'No, darling, don't argue. That's an order. We must not put the star anchor under stress—'

Of course, it was a dream, the lovely one from last night.

It was my first day in office after Rehan had returned. I had taken a month off from work, and so had Rehan, before taking up his Delhi posting. We went to our favourite spots, read books, and just got to know each other some more. Of course, papa thanked bhagwaan that Rehan was back and sent me a congratulatory SMS.

'You want to do something new?' Bunny asked.

'What do you have in mind?' I said.

Bunny was happy to have me back on the beat, but I was firm about the fact that I wanted a change.

'Try an art story, you know Samrat's sister, Sweety's sister-in-law, has gifted Sweety a rare Souza?'

'But didn't she get some expensive Hussains and rare Razas from her hubby as shaadi gifts?'

'Well, evidently the family is heavily into collecting art and it's their bahu's initiation,' Bunny said.

'Isn't art more Nandu's scene? Ask him,' I said.

'No! This should be a really bitchy piece.'

'Thanks for the vote of confidence.' I smiled.

'Baba, half the society types are Nandu's friends, he is not gonna bitch them out,' Bunny explained.

'What do you want exactly?' I asked.

'Bollywood heroine trying to fit into Delhi's uppity society circuit…'

'The card says Sweety is throwing a bash at her Bhondsi farmhouse and she is flaunting some old boys, haan? I saw the name of Zeeshan Haji from Dubai.'

'Okay, here's the thing, Sweety needs to do something to establish herself in Delhi's scene, all these society women are giving her the cold shoulder, you know. They invite her to their parties and gawk at her as if she is still a nautanki wali.'

Sweety was desperate to make her mark in Delhi's social circles. She wanted the world to know that she fit into Samrat's family, a family not only well known for their mind-boggling wealth, but also famous for their priceless art collection. Sweety's crash course in art had begun when Samrat started wooing her. He had introduced her to the world of Souzas and Razas and Raja Ravi Varmas. Interactions with her gallerist sister-in-law had only whetted her appetite. There were rumours that Sweety had acquired a few rare and frightfully expensive art pieces which she had hidden in her ante-room for privileged viewing on strict oath of secrecy.

So a cleverly planned launch party with the city's crème de la crème in attendance and TV channels and print media to record every groan and squeal of delight was Sweety's way of putting an end to her days in the social wilderness.

At first it did not look like a Bollywood crowd. Most of the women were elegantly dressed in stunning sarees, while the men were immaculately dressed in Zardozis, Jodhpuri bandhgalas and silk sherwanis. A performance by the band Earth Rhythms, with bamboo pipes and chimes, had the guests swaying to the melancholy notes. Sweety had paid special attention to the cuisine and there was something to suit every palate—from seekh kababs and continental salads to frozen fresh-fruit desserts and rum-soaked éclairs. But it was her drinks station and cigar counter that were the biggest hit.

Champagne and daiquiris, chiantis and clarets on one hand, and smoky cheroots on the other... the guests were having too much of a good time to bother about the masters hanging on the wall behind them or the really late show stoppers. The scene of action gradually shifted to the dining room where the layout, the menu and even the liveried waiters seemed straight out of a film set. The lavish dinner was complemented by chocolates and cognac.

After dinner, Sweety breathlessly interrupted the merry gathering and announced the arrival of the grand old man of Indian art, Zeeshan Haji.

Sweety clung to Haji possessively, shooting victory glances at the gawking women. The nautanki wali had socked the society ladies with her coup de grace.

I got my bytes from a gloriously happy Sweety, and was waiting my turn to interview the grand old master, all the while trying to think of prudent questions. After all, this was not a Bollywood actor.

Suddenly I was interrupted by the aggrieved and highly agitated artist Bharat Sehgal, who was also present at the showing. He came up to me and hissed, 'They are fakes! I have spotted five—but I am sure each and every one of them is a *fake*! What a cheat, such a *hoax*!'

I didn't get what he said at first. He was shaking my hand excitedly. I made him repeat every word slowly.

Bharat had spotted at least five fakes in Sweety's rare and priceless art collection. If Bharat was to be believed, the masters' collection that poor Sweety was gloating over was trash.

'I swear that work is not by Binoo Ghosh. He was my mentor, I would know.'

'Hello! How do you know? What's the proof?' A part of me didn't want to believe that Sweety had been duped. Poor girl,

I felt sorry for her. She was from Bollywood; it felt as if she was one of my own.

'He was my guru, I know his work; these are not his strokes!'

Why Bharat waited for the press to come in if he already knew the truth was anybody's guess. I thought he wanted maximum publicity. In any case, no one was really complaining. The guests got an unscripted scandal they would tweet and gossip about for days and the press got their reality TV moment of the day.

After a moment of shocked silence, everyone started talking at the same time, and the reporters got on their phones. Sweety stood very still, while Zeeshan Haji's face did not reveal anything.

I had mixed feelings. This was a big news story. 'Top Bollywood heroine duped!' But with the big names involved, it was a tricky one. I begged Nandu to help me with the script.

'What a story! Wow!' Nandu sounded almost envious over the phone. 'Of course I will write the script for you. Send me the details now. You need to get bytes from… and… and look out for… he will only create trouble…'

Sweety had bought the fake paintings at the prestigious autumn auction. The catalogue with the fake Binoo Ghoshes had been in circulation for a month and no one had noticed that there were fake paintings being circulated, not even the artist himself. Except struggling artist Bharat Sehgal. Bharat had not only spotted the fakes, he had also got a confirmation letter from Binoo through email then and there that said, 'I never painted such utter trash in my life.'

Poor Sweety was the victim of a sordid fraud. But the actress was peeved and accused Sehgal of choosing the party to create a scene. She screamed bloody conspiracy.

'You are a horrible person! Why are you doing this! Who invited you to my party?' Sweety was ready to explode.

'Aap tameez se baat kariye!'

'Throw this horrible man out! Security! *Security*,' screamed the young bride.

An ugly spat broke out between Sweety and Bharat, which was finally put to an end by Samrat, who requested Bharat to leave the hall rather than disrupt proceedings further. This angered the artist even more.

'Rembrandt is believed to have produced about 300 paintings in his lifetime, but it is said that there are 3,000 Rembrandts floating around in the art world. So I wouldn't be surprised,' said Zeeshan Haji finally. He turned around and found me blocking his path with my mike to get his byte. The rest of the media was behind me. He said, 'Please add that I had not seen the work yet, or I would have known. I know Binoo's work. Of course this is not his. But you need a trained eye. From which TV channel are you, again?'

'EMTV, sir.'

'Oh, yes. H. Raami is an old friend, even your gutkha king has bought many of my paintings. How is he? Okay, don't edit out this bit, yeah?'

'Sure, sir.'

'Terrible, terrible!' said Kakkar, a gallerist and a page three regular. 'It's all about establishing provenance, you know. I too hadn't seen the work…'

'But weren't you planning to exhibit her collection for your winter session?' I asked.

'We have a proper system in place. We only exhibit work whose sources we can establish,' Kakkar said, sounding hugely relieved at what had been discovered.

It would not have been a big deal... if the fake had not been sold. But it had been sold and that too to a Bollywood actress.

'I am sending an OB. Please be ready for lives and I want guests—get me Sweety, Samrat, some artists—get that Bharat chap,' Bunny said.

'Bharat's been thrown out... you can send Indu after him.'

'This is the big story today, a 9 p.m. lead. It is on all the channels because it involves a Bollywood actress and a hysterical artist. Nandu is going to help you. It's your big story!'

Nandu sent an SMS just then. *Send your p-to-c.*

After talking to scores of artists and gallerists, I finally came up with some coherent lines for my p-to-c.

'Copyright Law forbids copying of works of masters for thirty years after his or her demise. Given the difficulty in authenticating works of art, it is clear that galleries, auction houses and artists themselves have to find new ways to combat art piracy, so that people like Sweety are not cheated.'

When I reached office, Nandu generously offered to do the edits on my whale of a story. I couldn't thank him enough. I finally reached home dead tired.

'Bunny asked you to rest? Oh god, she is mutating into a human!' said Rehan when I told him that Bunny had ordered me home.

I had sent multiple SMSes to Chiki to witness my first

outing in the art world. And papa too. Maybe seeing my face on a different, *decent* story would give him some peace. Rehan gave up trying to shake me out of my whale-of-a-story jitters.

I couldn't make sense of my video package at first. It just came and went. I stared wide-eyed as my story came on air. I could not understand what was happening—the story was over and I couldn't find my frigging p-to-c; it seemed to have been chopped off!

Fuck, I forgot to give Nandu all the tapes!

Shit, I forgot to tell Nandu about the p-to-c!

Some of the crucial bytes were missing. Where the fuck was my signoff? It was like a script gone horribly wrong.

There had to be an explanation. My fingers punched Nandu's number. His phone was switched off. Where was he?

Why had he chopped my beautiful four-minute VT with bytes, graphics and music p-to-c to a pathetic 1.12 seconds? Nandu, where are you?

'Isn't that Nandu?' Rehan pointed at the TV screen.

Of course it was Nandu. On air. Live. On an EMTV exclusive with Bollywood actress Sweety. And he had Bharat and Sweety and Zeeshan Haji on the show with him. There was no need for any explanation now.

The bastard had taken my story from me.

My big whale of a story was not even my story now. I watched, stunned. Nandu was repeating my p-to-c lines verbatim!

'Copyright Law forbids copying of works of masters for thirty years after his or her demise. Given the difficulty in authenticating works of art, it is clear that galleries, auction houses and artists themselves have to find new ways to combat art piracy, so that people like Sweety are not cheated.'

No wonder he chopped off my p-to-c.

'Rembrandt is believed to have produced about 300 works in his lifetime, but it is said that there are 3,000 Rembrandts floating around in the art world,' Zeeshan Haji was telling Nandu.

'You know, Nandu, despite efforts by galleries and auction houses to certify provenance and authentication, fakes continue to creep in. The art of the steal is a big deal, my friend,' Kakkar was opining.

Chiki texted: *Dude, nice story. But you should have done a p-to-c.*

'Change the damn channel, Rehan. Switch to Comedy Central or something,' I groaned, defeated.

Things would never be the same between Nandu and me.

On the Sets: Africa

Johannesburg glistened as if it was bathed in gold. It was my first encounter with the city of gold that had played brilliant hosts to the Cricket World Cup. I was in Sandton City, Johannesburg, to cover the South African Fashion Week where Bollywood's favourite fashion designer Loki was showcasing his Fall-Winter Collection. I was part of the global fashion media invited to record and report every strut. It was also my first overseas trip on the sets of a Bollywood film, the shoot of which I would be covering. It was Latika's first film, titled *Chitty Chitty Dhoom Dhoom*. And she had insisted that EMTV send me, or there would be no junket. I wasn't complaining. I was in Johannesburg!

Several hours ago, my cameraman and I had reached the IGI airport dragging heavy equipment, at least three hours prior to departure. Just as well, because clearing shooting equipment at customs for overseas shoots was always a nightmare—DVC pro camera, the firewire cables, the gun mike, the batteries, no matter how innocuous, somehow ended up looking highly suspect when viewed through an X-ray machine. After a lot of arguments and counter arguments with the chief customs officer, we were allowed to go.

The ride through Sandton City was fantastic—wide roads lined with giant flowering shrubs, rhododendrons, sweet-smelling evergreen myrtles, trailing periwinkles and fresh orange nasturtiums, gleaming structures and orderly traffic. The city was as breathtaking as the website had promised. Our guide Zubessha, a commanding six-foot-tall woman of African origin, read out a list of dos and don'ts. She instructed us not to disregard the instructions on the schedule which she distributed to the Indian press. I thought there were more don'ts than dos. Don't shop alone. Don't change any schedules without informing. Don't shoot without permission. Don't leave the hotel without informing people of your whereabouts. And the famous 'curfew after dusk'—don't go out after sunset.

We reached Jo'burg's world-class twenty-storey Sandton City Towers, where we had been booked in. Zubessha briefed us about the history of Sandton City, which was built in 1973 as a pioneer centre. And the shopaholic's dream—the majestic ten-storey interlinked Twin Towers East and West spread over 45,000 square metres of commercial space.

The ride in the deluxe bus could have been smooth except that I was feeling extremely jetlagged. As I rested my head on the seat's backrest, my eyes were drawn to intricate drawings of Africa's Big Five on the seats. I traced the rhino grazing on the grassland, the tiger drinking water, the leaping lion, the long-necked giraffe nuzzling its young, and the hippo's girth.

And then I threw up. I had been feeling pukish all morning and could not hold it off any longer; I threw up all over the seats.

'Must be the airline food,' Anou, the style editor from *Images*, suggested. But I suspected it was the bad salmon at the fashion week press conference in Delhi, my last assignment before leaving for Africa. The tour bus grinded to an abrupt halt, the first and only break in Zubessha's carefully laid-out plans for us. Ten minutes of fresh air and a mug of hot coffee later, we were on our way.

The bus stopped in front of Sandton City Towers in the heart of Johannesburg's business district. It was freezing. My luggage, which included four huge bags, did not help matters.

As a rule, for a TV reporter, there is always too much to lug around. How I envied the print reporters who sauntered about with their single travel bags, while I was still doing the inventory on my samaan!

Bag number one: a Sony DVC pro camera with a wide angle adaptor, one HP laptop to FTP my footage, three firewire cables, a Sony camera battery, a Sony lapel mike, a gun mike as backup, one freezelight, a Sony battery charger, tons of AV cable, twenty mini-DVC tapes and yellow rain cover.

Bag number two: make-up kit, shoes and lingerie.

Bag number three: dresses.

Where was the bellboy? Surely I couldn't be that invisible lugging these huge bags?

The thing is, I never just entered a hotel lobby. I tottered, even tumbled in, dragging a jumble of bags. Zubessha appeared, mortified that I was standing all alone in the lobby. She helped me walk up to an efficient-looking press coordination lounge. I asked for a non-ciggy room.

My room had the most stunning view of the city. But compelling though the city's sights, smells and the sounds, Jo'burg would have to wait. At the moment my body felt battered and I rushed to the bathroom to puke.

I felt better and finally gathered enough strength to look around the spacious interiors, the king-sized bed with a butter mattress I could drown in and the softest pillows in the world. The lemon-scented bathroom that I couldn't focus on earlier as I was busy throwing up was another thing altogether. I could live in a hotel like this forever.

I soaked in the mother-of-pearl bathtub for almost an hour. Stepping out of the tub, I wrapped a pristine white towel around myself and lay down on the bed.

That was when I noticed Swiss chocolates in the welcome basket next to the bed, complimentary energy drinks and protein bars. There were also two bottles of Zappa, a peppy east African welcome drink, and French red wine.

After an hour I went down to the restaurant. Dinner started with boerewors or lamb chops and pap, which was served with a delicious tomato gravy. I tried the South African staple meat, the biltong, and gorged on the soft ostrich biltong, called kudu. I washed down my food with Dawa, an east African brandy. I was terribly spoiled, rested and finally restored beyond belief.

Next morning, there was a mad rush of reporters at the fashion fittings. But years spent crushing and pushing fellow reporters in countless fashion weeks came to good use—I was a pro at this—and when push came to shove, I never held back.

After some serious jostling and elbowing, the concrete throng of persistent press gave way and I managed to hold my own. My cameraman Shivam looked at me with new-found respect.

The organizers were finding it difficult to manage the numerous and easily the noisiest Indian channels who were hankering for time with Loki.

We were next. Loki had draped his collection on south African and European models, impossibly skinny yet alive, and stunningly gorgeous. The dazzling models flirted unabashedly with the cameramen. 'Indiaah! Namastey,' said a model in mock courtesy.

'I love these girls, darling, my collection looks perfect on them,' Loki gushed. 'So many buyers. I have had fabulous inquiries, you know.' He was accompanied by the models, who were strutting, posing, breaking into impromptu jigs, all the while looking at the camera. Loki had clubbed the launch party of a new champagne with his preview show.

Tunty, the new show producer appointed by Bunny to oversee my African shoot, was SMSing furiously about my links. Tunty suffered from too many personality disorders, to begin with. At this moment she was going ballistic about my links, this after picking my brains about the run order for the night show the whole of last night. She was schizophrenic.

'Hey, Laila, you are not enjoying. Come here,' Loki shouted across the room. Standing next to him was a model wearing what looked like an acrylic wig, diamante butterfly specs and two-feet-tall heels embedded with Swarovski crystals.

My earlier plan to indulge in the tempting tea spread had to be scrapped. Priority number one now was to go to the location and record the anchor links. With Tunty on my back, I would always have to be a little faster!

'You are always in a tearing hurry,' Shivam accused. 'I can't do a shoddy job. Framing the shot takes time, you know,' he added self-righteously.

I couldn't believe it. This two-pronged attack set my nerves on edge every time—telling the producer to slow down and coaxing the cameraman to work faster.

'Then frame it faster! And excuuuse me, can we be on the same page here? In case you have forgotten, we have a deadline to meet,' I shot back, pointing at my watch. Watching Shivam's pinched face as he dragged himself to pack the equipment, I felt like Cruella de Vil.

As we rushed towards our location, the Nelson Mandela Square, I wondered at the person I was becoming. Had the story become less important to me than recognition in people's eyes? Had I not yet got over the misty-eyed emotional rush of my first byline? What sort of footprint was I leaving in the field of journalism? It was the wrong place and the wrong time to get into existential angst.

'You are going on company money—remember, it's not a paid holiday!' Bunny's stinging words rang in my ears and brought me back to reality. Nelson Mandela Square: I had to shoot my links.

As we crossed Liberty Theatre, 'This is nice spot for links...' Shivam offered and I agreed without arguing, even though I thought it was a bit crowded and the NATs of the location were way up and would interfere with my audio. I scouted the location, which offered enough choices of backdrop for the best elements. A sulking cameraperson is a reporter's worst enemy and I did not want it to affect my shoot. I offered Shivam a can of energy drink as a truce, which he promptly refused.

'Do you think we should try the galleries?' I asked. 'Too dull,' said surly Shivam. 'There are also these designer boutiques and curio shops, even that cosy coffee corner… It should look Africa… that location looks like a can-be-anywhere.'

'Okay, so the opening link can be with Mandela in the background,' I pointed at the huge Mandela statue towering over us in the square, 'that's Africa enough.'

An African-style restro-bar built in a flashy Canary Wharf style with arresting melrose arches caught my attention. I walked into the exquisite interiors; there was a balcony restaurant overlooking the bar which would make for a catchy setting. The waterfall-like arrangement on one of the walls, hookah pipes and colourful cushions made me feel as if I was inside a souk.

'I think I have found the place where I will be doing most of the show links,' I said to no one in particular. Francis, the restro-bar owner, was more than happy to accommodate us but he had a special request. 'You must interview Beatrice, our star cook—she is the best cook this side of the world.'

Francis indicated the menu printed on a massive twelve-foot wooden panel that had items such as 'Moroccan tajine', 'saucy African oxtail stew', 'sea urchin gonads', 'horse hoof' and 'samosas'.

'Very much like your Indian samosas!' he added. 'And we also want you to get an interview with the manager.' He pointed at a toothy chap rubbing his hands next to the counter. I did not see any point explaining to Francis the logistics involved in FTPing footage in time for tonight's show. So I just played along till I banked the anchor links. Leaving Shivam to sort out the lighting issue, I went to the restroom to ready myself for the show—I had chosen a golden bustier and hurriedly dabbed on Mac Studio base and golden-bronze eye shadow. There was no time for the double coat of mascara or the rose blush-on but I applied some extra lip gloss. I silently thanked my mother's side of the family for my high cheekbones, which gave my face a kind of naturally made-up look.

Thankfully, the links were a breeze. I also did a few generic open-ended ones that could be fitted to mostly any story (as a rule, the generic links are very valuable for the producer packaging the show as they help to replace links that may have audio or video glitches).

There were just three hours left and ideally I should have been on my way to the hotel to send the feed, but the hotel IT department had assured me of a superfast one-minute clip per twenty-five minutes FTP speed.

When will you begin the feed? Tunty texted.

Am wrapping up, I texted back.

But surely you should have wrapped up by now! Tunty just didn't give up.

It is bizarre how some people think that just by asking the same question hundreds of times they will miraculously get an answer. Even more bizarre was how far removed from reality desk producers like Tunty, who often had no idea about the actual logistics of field reporting, were. I signalled to Shivam to pack up but I think he had started having too much fun with taking cutaways.

'We have to wrap up now.'

'I don't want anyone to point any fingers at me…' Shivam had begun his familiar wail.

Shit, no way was he starting his randi rona.

'Oh, for god's sake, man, can you stop taking this personally?' I exclaimed. 'What's the point, if all this splendid work does not make it back in time?' The rapidly setting sun had begun to increase my panic. 'What about your noddies?'

'Screw them. They have cutaways of the locations, don't they? Let Tunty sort it out.'

It was dark by the time we got back to our car. The driver drove through the near-empty streets, and in less than an hour delivered two exhausted and drained-out specimens to the hotel.

Finally a free bird, Shivam started humming. He was done for the day and all his equipment was packed. Finally he could go shopping with his friends from the other channels. Before leaving, he dumped his camera and firewire cables, the shoot tapes and video monitor in my room so that I could FTP in peace.

FTP Trauma

I ordered room service and settled down to a long night of FTPing, praying for good internet speed. Tomorrow was an early day as I was heading off to the sets of *Chitty Chitty Dhoom Dhoom*.

And then the nightmare began. I had my FTP process memorized and ready on hard copy but the damn laptop would not start.

I tried everything. I changed the adaptors, the firewire cables, unplugged the battery, then put it back, all in vain. The icons next to the Bluetooth one and the power button kept blinking like crazy but the display monitor was dead.

I called the hotel IT guy Mbali Jama but after half an hour of tinkering, all he came up with was a case of incompatible memory chips. Oh lord.

I had called the IT guys back in India but my word-by-word narration of what I was doing only created more confusion.

'Did you plug the laptop to the camera while the camera was on?'

'No!'

'Are you sure?'

'Yes!'

'Can you switch off and switch on the whole thing again?'

'I have switched it on and off several times, it's just not going anywhere. Please hurry, I have tons of footage to send.'

'Can you give it to the IT guy?'

By the time they had figured out what was wrong and got things working it was 2 a.m. When I sent the stuff it was already past four. I must have been sleeping pretty soundly when at 4.55 a.m. I was jolted awake by Tunty's phone call.

'What's your slug name? I have been waiting for you to send it to me for hours!'

Tunty had been put on night vigil too, and had not bothered to re-check my latest mail on the status of the feed. I didn't even have the energy to holler.

On Location

'The faster you shoot today, the faster you get to your shopping, Shivam!' My attempt at cracking jokes hit a sore nerve.

'Kya shopping! Scrooge in accounts has slashed my DA to bloody twenty-five dollars a day—is it a joke? Are we beggars?'

DA, or dearness allowance, is something of a staple discussion, a hot topic on long flights; it gathers momentum at transit stopovers, or while sharing 12,000 rupees worth of knee-cramping back-numbing economy seats; it is loudly discussed at red-carpet events, and cursed and bitched about during chill-out sessions in hotel rooms. This time the session happened on the sets of *Chitty Chitty Dhoom Dhoom*.

'Same story here, but you must have got some of your own too.' I wanted to avoid a long cribbing session.

'Other channel crew have producers travelling as well—the anchor and cameraman finish work and hand over their tapes to the producers, but here, you and I are still slogging like donkeys,' Shivam complained bitterly. My eyes glazed over and I stifled a huge yawn.

It was a small scene in the film and I remember wondering whether it would even see the light of day. That it would be released fast and sink even faster was something that, surprisingly, no one guessed at the time. With tapes and schedule and question list in hand, I stumbled into the set.

It was a lovemaking scene between Latika and Chimmy, and Chimmy just wasn't getting it right. A simple two-line scene had no business being stretched to so many hours. The accents (Chimmy's Hindi and Latika's English) were bizarre. Something or the other was going wrong all the time, be it the pose, the lights or something else.

'Who made him an actor?'

'What sort of name is Chimmy? Kutte par naam rakha hai?'

'His father is a big actor. He has always said that my son will study in Boston University and do an MBA. Boston gaya bhaad mein—ab papa wants his little Chimmy to be Shah Rukh!'

But one thing was clear: whoever had rented this place for the shoot was not charging by the hour. Many wasted hours later, when I could take it no more, I rushed out for a breath of fresh air, leaving Shivam to indulge in his fetish for cutaways. It could well have been a small impromptu claustrophobic set in Filmistan and my stomach was acting up again. I was afraid I would throw up if I allowed myself to remain inside the oven-hot film set any longer. Doing the outstation on the sets was not turning out to be as much fun as I had imagined.

For one thing, the double-storey hall that had been converted into the set was too depressing. Miles and miles of black cloth had been draped over almost everything. Back home, at least the assistant directors, set boys and unit hands filled me in on the latest gossip. And there was always someone whose sole mission was to feed me every thirty minutes, which made the grubbiest of Bollywood film sets bearable.

Here there were too few unit hands doing far more than their set of duties to bother with me. The director was reclusive and the food inedible.

'There are big fat machchars here, imported from Mumbai Studios,' Shivam complained, scratching himself furiously.

'Did you get cutaways?' I asked Shivam.

'I have the cutaways... You look very pale,' Shivam observed.

'I am not feeling well—let's bag Chimmy and bum it!'

Shivam and I smiled at the way that came out, but a startled Chimmy, who had just made an entry for his slotted interview, missed the humour. I rushed through the question list with Chimmy, by now sick and embarrassed. Like clockwork precision, the shoot was interrupted by a shouting match on the phone with Tunty, who was daft enough to slot newbies Chimmy and Latika for half an hour.

'You know, it's idiotic to have half an hour with these two,' I said.

'That's the thing, you reporters think the desk people sitting here are idiotic. By the way, did madam Laila deign to do Disha's show's links yet, or is that too much to ask?'

'Tunty, trust me when I say that no one wants to see

Chimmy and Latika. Both are newbies.' I was seething. 'And why the fuck do you want me to do Disha's show? What happened to Disha?'

'She had a face spa done.'

'So?'

'So she can't anchor for ten days—facial skin is very sensitive.'

'Arrey, but where do I have the time?'

'Make time.'

Fights between desk and field reporters happen routinely. Especially when the desk feels that the reporters are having a whale of a time at outstation shoots and the reporter assumes that the desk is a pit of nincompoops without the balls or brains to make it to the position of reporter.

Tunty hung up and the shouting match continued through terse SMSes.

Can we expect something today? Tunty texted. (Read: How much more fun will you have on company money?)

Bagged Chimmy, etc., will uplink, I texted.

Separate half an hour from the set, Tunty said. (You bloody well do it!)

But nothing happened on the sets. It's really boring, I texted.

Do your links from inside a landmark building, Tunty texted. (I will make you slog.)

We don't have permission, I texted back.

So get permission! trigger-happy Tunty shot back.

Okay. I will try!

Well, if you don't feel like doing it.

Hey, that's not it. Okay, let's see what I can get.

Tunty's new diktat meant I had to patao the actors into some sort of night out. A visit to a typical African curio shop seemed a good idea—the actors would have their fun shopping and I would bag my half-hour. We headed for an African bazaar overlooking Zoo Lake with the actors and some members of the crew.

At the African curio shop, Latika was particularly fascinated by the intricate beadwork, ethnic gold and silver as well as delicately crafted African jewellery, the kaftans and skins of game animals.

'Some genuine little pieces of Africa! The rest I will buy in Dubai,' she gushed. Her logic escaped me, but I was happy for her.

'Shivam, get the actors with colourful African artifacts and gigantic masks in the backdrop.'

'Leave that to me, na,' Shivam said. I think the actors' shopping spree reminded him of all the shopping he would miss out on. 'Bloody fucking Scrooge…' Shivam cursed the DA-slashing office accountant again.

So we shot and took bytes while the actors shopped and stopped for a bite at Moyo, a lovely intimate restaurant serving African food. The stars settled around the braai and chisa nyama barbeques. There were sweet and crunchy mielies and Ethiopian spiced ghee and gari, egusi, cizakis or daddawa. There was grilled sole, juicy steak, succulent oysters and fresh kabeljou. Some of the crew members were not as ecstatic with the offerings and grumpily settled for safe African samosas and Kenyan tea. After a good one hour, we wrapped up and bid the stars goodbye.

'With this DA what do I eat?' Shivam said accusingly, as if I was the DA slasher.

'Let's grab some decent burgers from Steers. Or do you want Peri Peri chicken from Nando's?' I asked. 'I have read there is some excellent takeaway coffee in Vida e Caffe...'

We got into the car to go back to the hotel to uplink the footage. But it was not to be our day. Our speeding car was stopped just outside the hotel by a stubborn traffic cop who refused to be impressed by our international media credentials. Our crime: we were in the backseat without any seat belts.

The burly cop was determined to drag Shivam and me to the station right then. After a lot of pleading and bargaining, he agreed to let us go when we coughed up 5,000 rands. I choked as my DA disappeared before my eyes into the pocket of the cop. But considering the alternative, it was money well spent. Imagine having to explain to Tunty why I couldn't send the night show's links—because my cameraman and I were in lock-up.

Item Hai!

Shivam and I ambled down South Africa's stunning Constantia district singing 'D.K. Bose'. Constantia lay in one of the greenest, leafiest parts of Cape Town, where stately homesteads, long driveways and oak-lined streets spelt old money and style. Shivam and I were to join the crew of *Chitty Chitty Dhoom Dhoom*. An item number was to be shot with Latika in the backdrop of the fertile Constantia valley.

The country lanes and horses and green belts seemed more ideal for walking a dog or stretching one's legs than for a Bollywood item number and TV anchor links. This place was famous for its wine—Chenin blanc, Cabernet Sauvignon, sweet Shiraz, sour Sauvignon blanc, Chardonnay, Merlot and Pinotage—and I was dying to savour all of them.

'This is the area that Simon van der Stel, first governor of the Cape, chose to cultivate and develop in 1685,' our guide duly informed us, the tourists. I took a moment to sit down and wondered at the ethereal beauty of South Africa.

Latika was still practising her steps when we reached the location of the shoot. She had been in the news for her topless calendar shoot and this was her first full-fledged dance item, a song called '*Angoori ki jawani ka achaar… sau hazaar lakhon bimaar*'.

Obviously Latika's charms were working. She had managed to bag a sexy item number in Dhanraj Sukhani's comedy film. Alongside, a role that required her to deliver dialogues. She was ecstatic.

Lattoo was trying every trick in the trade to get herself noticed and now wanted her film to be timed perfectly with her topless caper. At least no one would accuse her of not trying.

'People will be shocked when they see my pictures in the calendar! And how far I've gone,' Latika informed me, breathless from practising her steps. 'I am not being pompous, but I always push the envelope. You wait and see, every guy will have Maya's calendar in his bathroom,' she said as she swirled to the beat, revealing her ample cleavage.

Since the Constantia vineyards were a mere twenty minutes from the city centre, the plan was to visit all the farms in half a day, or set aside one whole day. Latika was quite excited about the trip.

We shot her amid sweeping views of Groot Constantia nestled in the heart of the Constantia valley, then the Klein Constantia, located in the foothills of the beautiful Constantiaberg mountains offering spectacular views across the valley with False Bay in the distance.

I uplinked the footage well in time to avoid any interaction with Tunty and preserve my own sanity. There I was, sitting in front of a vineyard in Africa in a thin silk outfit, with full make-up on at 1.45 a.m. and shivering. I was waiting for the OBs to wrap up when I got a call from Rehan.

'Remember your pregnancy test that had come negative?'

'Yeah.'

'Well, the hospital called.'

'Yeah.'

'They said it was a mix-up.'

'Yeah?'

'It's positive.'

'Meaning?'

'Meaning, babe, *we* are pregnant.'

'What? How can that be!' I asked idiotically.

'Well, it has happened the usual way!' Rehan sounded so happy that I did not have the heart to tell him about the ice-rink falls and the cans of Red Bull I had been guzzling, the heavy equipment I was lugging around and the fact that my cameraman was a chain smoker. My cursing the blasted hospital and threatening to sue it got Rehan thinking that perhaps I was having second thoughts about the baby.

There was a new SMS from Tunty: *Kuchh naya taaza? Any maal for tomorrow?*

I promptly burst into tears.

On Hold

How was I supposed to feel?

For better or worse, my life was about to change completely and irreversibly.

On my way back to India, a book called *Pregnanzy* caught my eye at the airport lounge. Then *Hello Mummy, Welcome Baby* and *Yo Prego, Ready or Not*—hell, there was a whole stack of them.

Three words, 'you are pregnant', had sent me scrounging through a book rack looking for titles I would never have imagined having anything to do with me. From being worried about Tunty and Bunny and Latika and Shivam and H. Raami and Nandu, it was like a new window had opened up with vast quantities of unknown data waiting to be processed.

The prefaces of the books informed me that I was about to embark on the most momentous journey of my life; it would begin with a nine-month stopover and also include stupidity, long- and short-term amnesia, crying and sleeping fits, the inability to keep food in my mouth and violent mood swings. I was pregnant. And I was freaking out.

I was prego. Pregnant. Preggers.

What's the big frenzy for? For heaven's sake, that mosquito is laying eggs right now, and look at the chimpanzee holding her newborn… I had to get out of the stupid bookstore.

'Attention slut, you are whipped.' Chiki's Facebook comment did not make me feel better. But it was nice to hear from her.

Nandu's comment: 'Preggers, already? But you still don't have your dream show!'

Latika's 'I will name her' was sweet.

And Bunny's 'I am the godmother' made my eyes moist.

Rehan received me at the airport, all protective and possessive. When he saw me he smiled, his eyes warm and unreadable.

Dude!

What do you do when you meet the father of the little thing inside you? I was feeling sad for the boyfriend I was leaving behind, but meeting this first-time-father for the first time was quite something.

We smiled and hugged, and smiled some more. Rehan would never admit it but he had tears in his eyes.

'You know, na? We are getting married.' He proposed in the car with my head resting on the small pillow next to the window and my legs on his lap.

Whatever the reason—whether it was because of the baby, or because he had finally accepted that the relationship had to be taken to the next level—I was too tired to argue. For the time being, that is…

Touched Up

It is common that on any special occasion, such as the production of a magical effect for the first time in public, everything that can go wrong will go wrong. Whether it's due to malignity of matter or the total depravity of inanimate things, whether the exciting cause is hurry, worry, or what not, the fact remains.

— NEVIL MASKELYNE, BRITISH MAGICIAN, 1908

'You actually did that, Laila?' Chiki asked.

'Yes! I wore the top back to front on air, *live*, while interviewing Hrithik Roshan! And for the sake of *continuity*, Bunny made me complete the whole show dressed like that.'

I was speaking to Chiki more often now. It scared me to think how close we had come to losing her. Chiki did not mention Amar Kapoor any more. But I was still mad at him. Rehan, however, saw it differently.

He did not think it was Amar Kapoor's fault. In fact, he said we should stop seeing Chiki as a babe in the woods. He felt bad for her but was pragmatic when it came to blaming Amar. I was initially hurt when Rehan blamed Chiki for being so starstruck that she could not see beyond the shine. He said it was impossible for a girl like her to have missed the telltale signs. He also thought that Chiki wanted out from her life, from her over-possessive mother and her twenty-four-seven existence. Amar Kapoor was the ticket to her escape. Yes, she had been shortchanged but could you blame Amar alone? She had had many chances to return, but she continued to pursue him.

But I thought Chiki deserved better. A friend of Bunny's had helped Chiki get a job in a production house. She was not making as much money and wanted her EMTV job back, but at least she was not at the mercy of friends.

'I saw your new promo. It's cool…' Chiki said.

My new promo said, 'Dump the newspaper that lands on your doorstep with a thapaak. Trust us, we will give saare desh ki khabar fataafat! Long live *Top 10 Speed News*.' Of course, the promo's first airing had Indu flipping out. 'But others are also making a significant contribution. Why is only her mug on the promo?' I chose to ignore her.

'Your intern, what's her name? That Pinky Mehta—yuck, babe, who did her make-up last night?' Chiki asked. 'She looked like a costumed harlequin, ya!'

'Please send feedback to EMTV.com. You can type your message and send it to 88888. The winning entry will…'

'What should I write in the feedback? Chiki asked.

'Maybe, why does EMTV have a monkey on air!' I said. 'Achha listen, Martina is beeping, I have to go for my make-up for the 7 a.m. roll…'

Morning shifts were my way out of the sleep-deprived state I was currently in these days—my body's reaction to pregnancy. The problem was that getting up at four in the morning was not normal, and my body knew this. The trill of the alarm clock repeatedly in the darkness—It's 3.55 a.m., time to get up! It's 3.55 a.m., time to get up!—drove me mad.

I had been told it would take a month or two for my body to get used to morning shifts, and not be tired every second of the day. And that after the first couple of months it would get easier. But going to bed hours earlier than the rest of the world was difficult.

I reached the station promptly at 5 a.m. every day. Make-up gods would wait to transform my face into broadcast quality. It's not like I wanted my very own *je ne sais quoi* effect on people… but trust me, you didn't want to see my 4 a.m. face on air. But there were some perks with the morning hours. It was the best time to get the latest in-house gossip. The make-up room was a hot bed of the most colourful stories.

As I settled down for my turn, in came an important anchor from the news desk who never had a minute to spare. She had been poached recently from another channel at an obscene salary.

'Hurry up, hurry up, just puff me up and I am good… I don't have a minute to spare,' she said.

'But that won't work! Your skin is looking sallow, your hair is all over the place. When did you wash it last?' Martina asked.

'Arrey, just do it… I have to go, I am late.'

Everyone in the make-up room just clamped up till she who never had a minute to spare left the room… but only after forty-five minutes of supreme primping with full make-up on.

'Fast, fast.' Martina found her voice after she left. 'She wants no make-up but goes for the complete work… gloss bhi, base bhi, thick eye shadow bhi… and then she says she does not need make-up.'

'Yaar, she should at least wash her face at home and come… it's so icky!'

Martina and her gang, which comprised Sunita, Faizal and Tony, were the sole reason why EMTV anchors looked the way they did. The make-up artists had the unenviable job of filling the wrinkles, ironing out the jowls and creating contours. Martina's brush was the magic wand that transformed anchors.

'Please don't open your eyes—let me apply eyeliner, then let it dry… we don't want your make-up to streak,' Martina warned as she carefully applied blue eye shadow to my closed eyes.

The door opened and I got a whiff of very expensive men's cologne. A star had walked in.

'Sir ka make-up karo.'

'Kaun aaya hai?' I asked. Martina did not answer.

The chair next to me squeaked as someone settled into it.

I opened my eyes to tiny slits and a beaming Amar Kapoor came into view. I am not often flummoxed. But there I was, sitting with my mouth open, staring at Chiki's lost knight; Kapoor too, it seemed, hadn't recognized me with my hair pinned up and make-up down.

'Hi there!' he said, giving me his most charming you-fan-me-superstar smile.

'Hello,' I said.

'Have I seen you before? No, must be on TV,' Amar tried to recall.

'Amar, there you are—let's go through the drill, shall we?' Rene Chaddha burst in with a very nervous sidekick holding a sheaf of papers that looked like questionnaires. Rene snapped her fingers and the sidekick handed her the papers nervously.

My eyes were suddenly smarting, and I winced in pain. The mascara had made its way inside.

'Shut your eyes now,' screamed Martina, 'lemme clean up. Tony, get me the eye drops—how much time for your show? Still an hour… you will have to close your eyes—what? Yes, you may talk on phone but eyes closed,' Martina warned as she placed thick cotton wads over my eyes.

I shut my eyes, my mind made up. I punched some random numbers.

'Okay, Chiki, what is this big star exposé you were talking about?' I said loudly. 'Chiki, pipe down. Why are you so angry? Which actor are you talking about?'

That got his attention.

'You have proof? What proof? *What did you do?* Oh my god, you taped him?' Of course there was no one at the other end, but what the heck.

Amar Kapoor sat very still.

'But Chiki, it is a big star, right? So who will broadcast it? Shit! What? You will put it up on the net—but what the fuck does it have, girl?'

Did our hero turn pale?

'But won't that compromise your—what? Which reality

show has given you an offer? You will reveal all on the show? What? You have *already* done it?'

Amar Kapoor choked on the ozonized water that he was drinking, specially imported from Europe for him, and jumped up.

He had had enough. As he stormed out of the room, I could hear Rene screaming and running after him. 'How can he go, is he mad? Get me his fucking PR. Hi, Amar sweetie, what happened? No, but you know you promised me... *Hello, hello...* the bugger has disconnected the phone. The fucker had a commitment! Is he zonked out? Get me someone else for the show. I will fuck his happiness.'

'Can I remove this cotton now, Martina?'

'O, haan haan! Your eyes have cleared! But sorry, babe, you missed the big drama—that's your punishment for not keeping your eyes closed,' Martina said petulantly.

'Sorry, Marty!' I was not sorry at all. And I did intend to keep my eyes open—wide open.

Wars

The fall of Gaddafi, the rise of Anna, hurricane Katrina devastating America… We were immersed in a lot of news when Delhi Fashion Week started. Several Bollywood stars and World-Cup-winning cricketers had promised to be show stoppers in the week-long glitzy affair.

So what was the possible connection between Gaddafi, Anna Hazare, Katrina and the fashion week? I was stupid enough to ask the news desk.

'There are buyers from Bahrain? Lots of Middle East presence, so get bytes on what they think of life after Gaddafi.'

'There are two designers from Korea, na? Get their reaction on the Gangnam mania! Better still, make them do the Gangnam dance.'

'Let's find out what your models know about Anna Hazare. Listen I want their bytes on Kejriwal's fashion statement, like aam aadmi ka fashion…'

'Get congratulatory bytes on the World Cup. Do they think

Bhajji and Basra make a good couple? Will Zakh and Isha marry? Does Yuvi make a better jodi with Preity or Kim?'

And then...

'Did we have a wardrobe malfunction today? Ramp par koi nanga hua?'

'Did anyone trip? Fall? No fashion bloopers?'

'Any superstars? Anyone glamorous will do—sports star, cricketer show stoppers, some hot sexy models!'

'Let's have that trend of men wearing skirts, na... people want to watch some funny weird fashion...'

'Give me the top five absolute fashion howlers... the common man does not want to understand good fashion, ya, people want to see high-fashion clowns! Give *sexy copy*... After all, it is the latest circus in town, right?'

Note: the stress was on weird, comic, bizarre, vulgar and philistine.

You had to hand it to Bunny, she cut to the chase, and fast.

And then there was Pinky Mehta, a treasure trove of labels.

Flaunting her recently purchased Dior clutch, Pinky strutted purposefully across the wobbly maidan at India Fashion Week, her freshly cut Fendi goatskin pumps making squeaky noises. She casually dropped her Burberry coat and allowed us to make noises at her exclusive Hermès scarf before she stuffed it disinterestedly into her flashy Louis Vuitton handbag. She crossed our OB spot, reeking of expensive Chanel, or was it an Yves Saint Laurent perfume, flashing her Bvlgari jewellery as she waved her Movado time piece attached to an overripe arm at someone.

Pinky's fixation with foreign labels was as irritating as it was fascinating. On the first day of the fashion week in Delhi, Pinky's outfit screamed lunacy from top to bottom—a preposterous lace and braid shirt (from London's Marc and Jacobs, she cooed importantly) teamed with a bizarre flouncy skirt (from Dolce and Gabbana, she insisted). She had been aptly nicknamed Pinky Pansy.

'Pinky babe, you are determined to bring the Queen back!'

'Laila, *this* is fashion… it's the latest collection to hit Harrods,' the queen of catastrophic kitsch informed me. Shrugging her masculine shoulders, which a nice Jill Sanders I-line top struggled to cover, a horribly mismatched golden and diamante studded bracelet on her wrist, she gave meaningful stares at my outfit.

'Oh my god, Pinky, your shoes are *alive!*' I said irritably, pointing at her hairy brown shoes. 'Guys, I think Pinky's sandals are wearing a *wig*! Why is she wearing her pet to fashion week?'

Pinky was something of a misfit in a group of hardcore TV journos. But I doubt she even considered herself a journo in the first place. 'What the fuck is she doing dressed up like a zebra? Iski toh main leti hoon,' bitched Sneha, my on-location producer, whose fashion sensibility was limited to fitted jeans teamed with what-she-grabbed-first from her wardrobe. She had been assigned to me by Bunny, who wanted to make sure I didn't do anything too adventurous in my condition. By now my baby bump had started showing but as the cameraman's focus was more on mid-shots when I was standing and doing the links, it wasn't visible on TV. I think everyone thought it was cool to have a pregnant hack running around and reporting fashion.

'Our little Aisha has strayed from her "fancy flock"… but nothing so serious that interning at a news channel can't fix!' said Sneha. 'Saali, I am looking like a dhoban now,' she complained while I quietly looked at my attire—a soft lemon-green one-shouldered Gauri-Nainika silk top and blue jeans and sneakers. 'I wonder where she is getting all the latest designer wear from.'

'Hey, Pinky,' a PR chick strutted over and crooned. 'Babe, I have something for you.' She gave Pinky a stunning silk limited-edition scarf, ignoring me and Sneha standing right next to her.

'Oh, you shouldn't have… listen, I absolutely cannot, ya! You are spoiling me,' she gushed even as she grabbed the freebie.

Pinky Mehta did not cover events like the rest of us hard-pressed entertainment reporters. She was invited to events and often stayed back longer than the rest of the hacks, talking to sufficiently important people. Soon it was only Pinky Pansy who got the invites. Needless to say, it led to a lot of heart burn on the desk.

'Laila, please help Pinky. She is your junior, you know. You need to train the next guard!' Bunny's words conjured ridiculous pictures of me guarding the fashion citadel and blocking Pinky's path in her rise to stardom.

'Ya sure, in fact, it was I who gave her contacts,' I lied.

❦

Rehan was going ballistic trying to tell me how unsafe and idiotic it was to continue active reporting in my condition but I couldn't just sit and twiddle my thumbs and let some second or third guard walk all over my beat, could I?

I had fixed up a backstage shoot—a behind-the-scenes with Bollywood's top designer Loki, who had promised that he would get a well-known actress for an impromptu style check. The hitch was getting there. There were beefy bouncers stopping us at every point regardless of our special 'gold' entry cards. And despite the squeaky clean carpets, the floors felt wobbly; there was only so much a durree covering a hurriedly flattened maidan, otherwise reserved for melas, could achieve.

I trudged the distance from the makeshift main showing area MSA1 to MSA2 and headed straight backstage.

As usual, I did not know at that time that I was walking into a big story.

When I reached backstage I was irritated to see Pinky already perched on a chair, giggling with the PR chick. I couldn't let a chit of a girl reign supreme on my parade, could I?

'Hello!' I said a little brusquely. 'Tum bhi ho? How come?'

'Loki has promised me an exclusive style check for my segment,' Pinky said.

Style check for *my* segment—dumb bitch!

'But I am doing it, na, sweetie!' I said.

'Bunny asked me to… you can ask her.'

'Yeh lo! No need—I am sure you will not make up such a thing. Anyway, I have to do a feature. Chalo, Shivam!' I signalled to my cameraman.

I was sure Bunny was only trying to help but I couldn't believe this babe was trying to walk all over me. The very thought stressed me out. And I had heard that pregnant moms who took the most stress gave birth to hyperactive and cranky kids.

'Kya karega? Feature hai?' Shivam said.

'No! Hum jayenge baahar,' I said.

Fuck the feature. Bunny did not want me to move my arse, so...

'I am shocked, stunned! Motherfucker is a thief! Woh chor hai, that bastard should be in jail!'

These words stopped me dead in my tracks. A hysterical Muneet Sharma was hurling the choicest of invectives at Loki. Before I could decide whether I wanted a part of this drama or not, Muneet saw me. I braced myself for a lecture on the pesky press poking their unwanted noses in everyone's personal affairs.

'Laila, Laila! Good you are here... just the person I wanted to see.'

Just the opposite of what I thought I would hear.

'I will tell you everything about the racket that is going on! And you...' he commanded his PR chick, 'go and get the rest of the press!'

'I am shocked. You have to forgive me... I am so emotional! I need some H_2O!' Muneet said, shaking. I was alarmed.

'I am stunned, those are my designs. It is so brazen. You'd think there are no rules in this country... there are laws, you know... this chunni worn by actress Tanuja Chatterji, this choli, they are *my designs*!'

He shoved a magazine with a photograph of a model wearing a red chunni and a bustier embedded with coins in my face.

'See, see—neechey kya likha hai! Loki! This is not Loki's! This is mine. It is so dishonest to claim it as your own. I did not even notice it. My friends saw this film and they said, hey, isn't this yours…'

Behind me the media was in a frenzy, each reporter restless to do his live presser. Cables were being laid and the dhakka mukki had begun. The reporters were anxious because they thought that Sharma would cool off before their turn came. But they needn't have worried. The entire drama, the ranting, the waving of the magazine, the threat of taking the legal route, was enacted faithfully for all the channels.

'I think we shouldn't be here in your state,' Shivam said, eyeing the swelling crowd.

'Ya, ya, just one more question,' I whispered.

Laila, do we have Sharma? Bunny's SMS interrupted my interview with the hyperventilating designer.

Yuss. Am doing him right now!

Send uplink—I want it in this cycle of the bulletin.

You will have to play straight from tape for that, there isn't much time.

Ya, ya, we will play straight from tape; it will get max play out.

The crème de la crème of society was slugging it out, washing their expensive dirty linen in public. The Muneet Sharma–Loki fight was the biggest headline of the day.

I was feeling tired and dizzy from all the excitement and the fact that the makeshift quarters backstage were cramped, didn't help matters.

On my way out to get some fresh air, I saw Loki with the actress while Pinky was standing quite close, all geared up for her interview. I butted in.

'Loki, can I get your reaction? Muneet is accusing you of pilfering his designs?' I said.

Loki turned two shades redder. The actress's smile froze and Pinky Mehta had a stupid look on her face.

'I didn't rip anyone off—we are all respectable people here, it was a genuine mistake,' Loki tried to laugh it off.

'But he is calling you "Loki the Ripper".' By now the media had collected around Loki. The actress was looking at her watch nervously and whispering to her PR person, who had just walked up. Obviously, she wanted no part of this drama. Pinky tried to get a word in, but no one was really bothered about her stupid style statement segment any more.

Loki sneaked into the venue to clear the air in front of the press. Suddenly he found a hundred mikes shoved in his face.

'I'm a costume designer… and as a film stylist, I can pick up stuff from anywhere. I will get credit in the film in which the stuff has been used.' Now, Loki was very much on the backfoot.

The media turned their attention to the beleaguered actress, who was caught in the wrong place at the wrong time.

'Whose costume is this? How do you know it is Loki's?'

'Apni latest film ke baare mein bataaiye.'

'You were seen at the Ajmer Sharif Dargah? What did you wish for?'

'You are an old friend of Loki. He has designed for many of your films—how will you defend him?'

Meanwhile, Muneet was going hammer and tongs at Loki. He played up to the gallery...

'Of course I am exploring my legal options,' Muneet confirmed. 'He calls himself Bollywood's favourite fashion designer... but he should work on his morals and ethics! It's difficult to patent a design... a pin here, a tuck there—he must have stolen my design templates and thought, if Bollywood stars endorse them the designs will become his—'

Loki suddenly interrupted Muneet's monologue and screamed, 'What bakwaas! Everyone knows who is copying whom! Your design was sourced from a boutique for the styling in my latest film and I would have given you the credit. What about the countless details you have copied down to the minutest stitch? From the villages? Just because the poor craftsmen you go to meet in the villages of Jaipur and Orissa don't know any better—you have been snitching and passing off their designs as yours for years!'

Muneet stared open-mouthedly at this accusation in front of the media. In the commotion I could see the Bollywood actress fleeing and stupid Pinky pleading with her to stay for her segment.

National TV notwithstanding, male designers can be pretty loud when they crib. Plagiarism accusations in the middle of fashion week! A hornet's nest had been stirred.

'Blatant lies...'

'What cheek...'

'Should I tell the press about the clothes you pick up from Bangkok and sell here at ten times the price, you criminal?'

Suddenly I could see the walls closing in on me and the ground coming up to meet me pretty fast.

I woke up in the hospital to a very worried Rehan and uncle… and papa!

'This has got to stop,' papa said.

'Welcome back! You gave us a scare,' uncle said.

'Don't panic, you are fine,' Rehan said.

'Copycats!' I finally responded.

'Huh?'

'My feed slug is copycats, can you please tell Bunny?'

'Wha—t?'

'Bunny ko please tell. It's important for the show…' I mumbled before losing consciousness again.

And Finally

Maya's film *Kaayapalat* was a huge hit. So was her item number, '*Angoori jawaani*'. She was nominated for several 'Best Fresh Face' awards. She was being offered obscene amounts to perform item numbers—in films as well as stage shows. Last I heard, Ronsher Khanna wanted to cast her in his next. TV channels were fighting for a piece of Maya, demanding her phonos and symsats and lives. EMTV had approached her to endorse a campaign. She had agreed.

Poor Bunny had to eat crow. Her resolve to ban Maya from EMTV had not cut much ice with H. Raami, who insisted that he wanted Maya, she being an ex-EMTVite and all that; a star endorsement with her would not harm the channel's reputation. Maya insisted that she would do the deal with Bunny only if EMTV wanted her to endorse the channel's latest campaign, 'Save the Butterflies'. So it was left to Bunny to get Maya signed on for the new campaign. Bunny was not too kicked about it but she did not have any option. Of course, she was sugary sweet when she requested Maya to endorse 'Save the Butterflies', her clenched fingers this side of the receiver notwithstanding.

Chiki rejoined EMTV for a while as Bunny had forgiven her quite a bit and said she could have her job back. But Chiki had made up her mind that she would join a TV production house. She was planning to go back to Mumbai with her mother, who had become really good friends with Bunny. In fact, the two were planning a holiday together. Indumati had resigned and was joining Q Channel as vice-president at ten times Bunny's salary. Indu had been given a grand farewell party after her notice period was over—Chiki danced wildly at the do, which annoyed Indu no end.

Bunny now wanted younger girls at the desk. And till my due date, I was on desk duty under Bunny's strict orders.

I was at the desk when she kicked for the first time. As if she was testing the waters. It was when Bunny opened her mouth to give some expert gyaan on child birth that the baby kicked like mad. I was so excited that I immediately told the others, and it freaked everyone out, especially Nandu. No one could believe that something like this could happen. Chiki clapped. 'Hey, Nandu, get ready for the kicks this one will plant on your backside,' she screamed.

Rehan was overjoyed. Aunty looked pleased as punch and she, along with Sheena, took it upon themselves to supply our home with baby goodies. Uncle too was very happy. Papa was delighted and couldn't keep the smile off his face. Probably pleased at the prospect of the impending domestication of the prodigal daughter whom he had almost written off. He could now dream of the perfectly decent civil services life for his grand-daughter or -son. Papa was not in favour of my continuing the job but that was just too bad.

Bunny and Chiki were with me during the delivery. Chiki held my hand and Bunny held the fort along with Rehan.

Lattoo kept sending huge caches of baby gifts till I had no place left in the house and requested her to stop the gifts. Then she sent me a truckload of diapers.

Nandu came armed with flowers and a sheepish smile. Indu did not even call.

I stared at her in awe. I wished I was living in a time when women did not have to do stuff to prove themselves to the world so that I could stay home all day and keep looking at her.

I named her Djiah, meaning 'song of the forest' in some African language, as it was in Africa that I had found out that I was pregnant.

It has been six months of gladness, sadness and madness.

One more thing: all the clichés about new parents being this and that... are hundred per cent true.

Roll Time

A breathtakingly sexy creature stares at me warily. She is
sitting at my desk, fiddling with my console. It is my
first day back at work, and here I am looking at my desk,
which feels empty with no Lattoo, no Indu and no Chiki.
Bunny has a larger cabin. Nandu has two new shows. Pinky
bailed out to take part in a fashion appreciation tour in New
York. And there are some sleek new additions.

'Isn't she cuddlesome? You should see the other maal Bunny
has hired!' Nandu whispers.

'She looks shit scared,' I say.

'Oh, that would be because we filled her in about you!'
Nandu winks at me.

'Lord, she looks ready to burst into tears! Did you tell her
I am a bitch or what?'

'Of course, that too!'

Bunny yells from her new cabin: 'Tina, this is Laila. Laila,
Tina. Where are the rest of the girls? Nandu, get them in!

Okay, girls, this is Laila. Your supreme lord for every waking hour that you spend in EMTV for the rest of your three months. She will make you cry, tough luck; she will fuck your happiness, too bad. Anytime you want to scream mummy, don't come running to me. There's the door. Hold Laila's bag, follow her around, do what she does and if you can manage to do even one-tenth, you still have a hope of a job at the end of the three-month training period. Now, meeting over. Get on your arses. Deliver.'

You still couldn't accuse Bunny of being too endearing.

'Three new perfectly formed maidens! Mommy, there is a whole bunch of them,' Nandu whispers.

Mommy? Mommy! Oh shit! Do I look too padded? I have to hit the gym after the show.

'And Laila darling, are you ready to roll?'

Acknowledgements

This book would not have been possible if I did not have the privilege of knowing the exceedingly exceptional and magnificent journalists in Delhi and Mumbai over the years in the most fiercely competitive beat that entertainment is.

I would like to thank Neelini and Bidisha for their tireless editing; Shuka for her incredible creativity. Thank you, Mita, for going through my initial drafts and pointing me in the right direction. I would also like to thank Karthika for her incredible faith, crackling wit and extraordinary generosity, without which this book would not have been possible.

I am indebted to the brilliant journalists and individuals I have met—Sonal Joshi, Aneesha Baig and CSP. Thank you for tolerating me at my worst.

Thanks to the one lovely girl for whom the world is not enough, little Radhika, who pushes me forward like no one else.

I am grateful to papa and Prashant for all kinds of important advice.

Thanks Yash, for ensuring that I pace myself and don't go off the rails... and for being a rock solid presence in my life.